THE TYRANT

BANKER #3

PENELOPE SKY

HARTWICK PUBLISHING

Hartwick Publishing

The Tyrant

Copyright © 2019 by Penelope Sky

CONTENTS

1

CATO

Weeks passed, and we didn't discuss what happened in Florence. Maybe she was waiting for me to say it, to whisper those words to her when she least expected it. That wasn't going to happen, so I was glad we didn't have to talk about it again.

I didn't enjoy hurting her.

But I wouldn't say it just to make her happy.

We were both asleep in the middle of the night when she became restless, kicking her feet and whimpering in her sleep. Then she jolted upright and rested her hand on her stomach. "God, do you ever stop kicking?"

My heavy eyes opened to take in her frame in the darkness. She held herself up with one arm while the other gently stroked her stomach. She breathed hard through the kicks, tensing up in a way she never had before.

I sat up and placed my hand over her stomach, but I didn't feel any kicking. "Baby, I don't feel anything."

"Well, I feel pain…"

All the sleepiness left my eyes, and I shifted into action. I got out of bed and pulled on the first pair of jeans I could find. I threw on a shirt and a jacket then picked out something for her. "Baby, get dressed."

"Where are we going?" She slowly rose to her feet, her hand still on her stomach.

"We're going to the hospital, just to make sure everything is okay."

"God, do you think there's something wrong?" She grabbed the clothes I picked out for her and quickly pulled them on.

"I'm sure everything is fine, but I'd rather be safe than sorry." I pulled out my phone and called my team to prepare the car. Then I had my security captain call the hospital before we arrived so they knew I was coming. Siena wasn't going to wait even a minute to be seen by someone.

I helped her down the stairs and out the front door.

She kept gripping her stomach. "It hurts."

"It'll be alright." I helped her into the back seat, and we finally drove off. I put the heater on full blast and then wrapped my arms around her. "I'm sure Martina is fine, Siena. Your body is going through a lot right now. Just remember that. It's probably normal."

"God, I hope so." She breathed hard as she gripped her stomach. "I couldn't handle it if something happened to her... She's everything to me. I love her so much." Her eyes filled with a sheen of tears.

My heart snapped in two. "I love her too. If she's anything like either of us, she's strong. She'll get through this." I held Siena close to me and brushed my lips along her hairline. I tried to do anything to keep her calm. Siena wasn't the type of person to respond emotionally to trauma, but the pregnancy clouded her pragmatism.

"I hope so..."

———

We got in to see the doctor right away, and after running some tests, they determined Siena was experiencing Braxton Hicks, a common occurrence in pregnant women. The contraction of the uterus was the source of her discomfort. She must have thought Martina was kicking because she was half asleep, her faculties slow.

"You're sure she's alright?" Siena asked as she sat back on the hospital bed, her hands on her stomach.

"Absolutely," the doctor reassured her. "But you made the right decision coming in tonight. The contractions should stop in a few hours. Try to stay comfortable until they pass." He walked out and left us alone in the room.

I kept a straight face because it was my job to stay calm, but the relief that washed over me almost made me weak in the knees. When she'd gripped her stomach like that, I'd feared something much worse was happening. The pregnancy had been a complete accident and I'd never wanted a kid, but Martina was such a part of our lives now, and I would be devastated if something ever happened to her.

Or Siena.

The tears welled up in her eyes again, wet and shiny.

"Baby, what's wrong?"

"Nothing," she whispered. "I'm just so happy she's okay…"

I placed my hand in the center of hers and kissed her forehead. "Me too. At least if this happens again, we'll know exactly what it is."

"I hope this is a one-time thing because it's pretty painful."

"The doctor said it'll pass." I took her hand and guided her off the table. She was five months along now, and her belly was getting bigger with every passing week. She'd switched to maternity clothes to keep her belly comfortable. "Let's get you home and in bed."

"Okay. Thanks for getting me here so quickly. I know you arranged all of that." She grabbed her clothes from the chair and slipped out of her gown. "Whenever I get scared, I know you'll make sure everything is okay."

I watched her lower her shirt over her head and then pull her sweatpants up her body. Instead of admiring her figure, I focused on her side profile. The only reason I'd spared her life was because of the baby growing inside her, but now I didn't just want to take care of Martina. I wanted to take care of Siena too, to protect both of them. "Baby, I'll always take care of you."

———

It was a cold December. Fog pressed against the windows downstairs in the kitchen, and the sky was constantly overcast. The walk from my car to the office always sent chills down my spine. The weather in central Italy could be so drastically different. The summers were so hot and humid that it could be unbearable, and the winters turned so cold that it almost snowed. If I had to choose, I preferred winter. It was too hot in the summer to wear my expensive suits.

Siena sat across from me at the dining table. She'd finished most of her dinner then sipped her water. Her belly was getting so big that she had to sit farther away from the table so she wouldn't accidentally bump it. "When are we putting up the Christmas tree? Christmas is a week away."

I finished my last bite of the salmon and washed it down with a sip of water. "We don't put up a tree."

Dumbfounded, she stared at me like I'd said something much worse. "Excuse me?"

"We don't put up any decorations."

"Because...?" Her eyebrow was still raised, and she looked utterly appalled.

"Because we don't," I said simply. "Never have."

"What's wrong with you?" she blurted. "It's Christmas. You have to put up a tree."

I never got invested in the holidays. My family got together for Christmas dinner and exchanged a few gifts, but we didn't make a big fuss about it. Christmas eve was the best night to pick up tail. Any woman in a bar on Christmas eve was depressed, and she fucked like being good in bed would fix all her problems. "Why?"

She threw her arms down. "Because it's Christmas. That's what you're supposed to do. I always have a tree up at my place even though there are very few presents under the tree. It's the spirit of the season."

"Well, you know I don't have much spirit."

"What about Giovanni and the rest of the staff? They'd probably like a tree."

"I don't care what Giovanni and the rest of the staff want. This is my house."

She rolled her eyes. "Grinch."

"What did you just call me?"

"Grinch," she said louder. "You know, that big green thing that lives in a cave alone and hates Christmas."

"Just because I don't put up a tree doesn't make me a big green hamster."

"He's not a hamster."

"Whatever." I drank my water again.

"Well, I live here too, and I want a tree." She turned to the kitchen. "Giovanni, you'd like a tree too, right?"

Giovanni's eyes moved back and forth between mine and hers, as if he didn't want to answer for fear of retaliation from either of us. "I need to check the oven..." He walked off.

"See?" I said. "He doesn't want a tree."

"Oh yes, he does. He just doesn't want to piss you off."

"Smart man."

"Cato, I want a tree." She looked me in the eye as she made her demand, using that sexy confidence to get what she wanted. "When Martina is here, we're going to have wonderful Christmases for her to remember. We're going to do it then, so we may as well do it now."

"Why is this so important to you?"

"Because my family always used to get into the spirit of the holidays. We would put up the tree together every year. Even Landon would help. Why are you so against it?"

"I'm not. It's just something I've never done. Never had time."

Disappointment filled her eyes. "What's the point of working so hard if you don't stop to enjoy it? If you doubled the amount of money in your account, would you really be happy? Or would you be unhappier because you'd realize that nothing makes you happy?"

She often made such sharp observations about my character, and they always made me reflect on who I was. It made me realize how lonely I was, how all the money and all the women in the world hadn't make me happy. So far, there was only one thing that ever made me smile—and I was looking at her. "It's not just about the money. It's about the accomplishment. It's about growing something you created."

"I understand that, but you're already on top of the world, Cato. Do you really need to grow it anymore?"

"If you aren't growing, you're stagnant. And if you're stagnant, that's a red flag."

"But when you're a multibillionaire, who cares?"

"It keeps everyone in line."

"That is way too much work," she said. "There's not enough money in the world to make me sacrifice my life like that."

"But it's given me the ability to take care of you, to give you a luxurious life that makes you feel safe."

Instead of being touched by what I said, she shook her head slightly like I'd said the wrong thing. "We could be living at my old place, and that would be just fine. As long as we have food on the table and electricity, our happiness would be exactly the same. You could do your share of the work by keeping me warm at night."

The memory of her house brought me an unexpected bout of longing. There was something about that cozy house I loved. It was simple, peaceful. My estate was a comfortable palace, but it lacked that quality. "Or I could fix your furnace."

"Like you know how," she teased. "And paying someone to fix it doesn't count."

"I have more talents besides making money."

"Like sex?" she asked. "I'll give you that."

That was quite a personal comment to make in front of Giovanni, but I didn't care.

"Back to the point," she said. "Let's put up a Christmas tree. That entryway is so tall that we could put up something big with lots of lights and decorations."

"I don't have any."

"Then we'll go buy them. Come on. Please?"

If this was so important to her, I wouldn't deny her. "I have work tomorrow."

"Whatever. Blow it off. When you're dead, you can't take that money with you. And your legacy, your daughter, isn't going to remember how much money you made. She's going to remember your laugh and your smile. She's going to remember all the time you spent together. You've conquered the business world. Now you need to focus on conquering the personal world."

———

We bought the biggest tree we could find. Thirteen feet tall, it was a tree that wouldn't fit into an average house. We picked out the lights and decorations from a holiday shop then went across the street to get hot chocolate.

She sat across from me at a table by the window, her eyes lit up brighter than the Christmas trees inside the windows of the shops. She had an ethereal glow that had nothing to do with the pregnancy. Her smile was so natural and infectious, bringing a warmth that was hotter than the hot chocolates in our hands.

I'd lost track of what she'd said because I was staring at her so intently. This woman had been the only one in my bed for the last six months. The longest I'd been with the same woman was two days. But now it was six months. That was half a year. I still had the urge to fuck her in the alleyway, still wanted to hop in with her in the shower, and still wanted to take her missionary so I could watch her face while I fucked her. Now I slept with her every night, and all the cuddling didn't bother me. I liked feeling her next to me because I knew exactly where she was, that she was safe.

"Cato?"

My eyes focused on the words coming out of her mouth. "Yes?"

"Some guy came up to the window and took our picture with a big camera." She pointed to the window, which had frost filling up the corners.

"Yeah, they do that." I hadn't been photographed in months because I never went out anymore. I went straight home after work, and my property was closed to the public so they couldn't see Siena inside. Now that we were out and about, shopping for Christmas decorations, it was the perfect opportunity to catch me off guard. "But you knew that already since you stalked me."

"And you just ignore it?"

I shrugged. "Nothing I can do about it anyway."

"Couldn't you threaten to kill anyone who publishes it?"

"It'll still circulate online. I could take everything down, but having those pictures still helps my image. If anyone wants to know, they'll see how fascinated the world is with me."

"Does the world know you're having a baby?"

"No. But I'm sure they'll find out soon enough." I didn't care about keeping that secret because it was simply impossible. People would find out one way or another. If someone really wanted to dig deep, they could find my trust and see who I was leaving my assets to. Martina Marino didn't exist, but it was easy enough to guess who that person was.

"Does that concern you?"

I shook my head. "It's inevitable."

She took a drink of her hot chocolate, looking stunning in her long-sleeved red t-shirt. It fit the curve of her tits nicely. As her pregnancy progressed, her boobs got bigger. They also got firmer, rounder. Her nipples were two irresistible diamonds. The size of her hips and thighs increased, but that didn't bother me. She'd always been on the slender side, so now she was filling out nicely. My attraction for her was growing to dangerous proportions. Men always complained about how fat their women got during pregnancy, but now I didn't understand it one bit. There was nothing sexier than watching your woman's body grow your child. Her curves were more pronounced, and her figure was fuller. It turned me into a more sexual man than I'd been before.

She watched me stare at her. "What?"

My mind came back to reality. "Just looking at you."

"But you had this look on your face..."

I shrugged. "Because I can't believe how beautiful you are."

―――――――

Giovanni seemed even more excited to decorate the tree than Siena was. "These ornaments are beautiful. You did a great job picking them out, Mr. Marino."

"That was Siena." I'd just agreed with everything she showed me.

Giovanni stood at the top of the ladder and added the ornaments on the branches.

Siena decorated the bottom part of the tree because she wasn't allowed to use the ladder at all. "It's already looking so beautiful."

I attached the ornaments to the hooks before I handed them to her, letting her choose where they went. I found it more entertaining to watch Siena walk around anyway, especially when her back was turned to me and her ass looked incredible.

It took us several hours to get the tree completely decorated, especially since Siena and Giovanni wanted it to be perfect.

The entryway into the house was so large that it actually looked better with the Christmas tree as the focal point. It filled the space nicely, like it should be there all the time.

When it was completed, Siena stepped back to admire the twinkling lights and the shiny ornaments. She crossed her arms over her chest and stared at her handiwork.

Instead of looking at the tree, I looked at her. I watched the glow in her eyes, the way her happiness shone brighter than the lights on the Christmas tree. Little things like this made her the happiest, not the expensive cars in my garage or the designer suits in my closet. She cared about the little things in life, moments she would remember forever.

————

She poked her head out of the bathroom, hiding most of her body from view. "Thanks for shopping with me today."

I sat up in bed, naked under the sheets and ready for sex. "It wasn't as bad as I thought it would be."

"You had fun and you know it." She continued to keep her body out of my line of sight. "I got something for you today. Picked it up when you were paying for the ornaments."

"An early Christmas gift?"

"You could say that." She stepped out in red lingerie—a push-up bra, a thong, and red stockings to match. Her pregnant belly was unobstructed, round and sexy like the clothing she wore. To top it off, she wore a Santa hat.

All the air left my lungs, and I lost my ability to speak. It was so unexpected, and that made it a million times better. My cock had already been hard because I knew sex was coming, but now he was so thick it hurt. My balls tightened like they wanted to release my seed already. "Fuck, I love Christmas."

She crawled onto the bed then moved on top of me, her pregnant belly beautiful. When she sat on my lap, she removed the Santa hat and placed it on my head instead.

I was too aroused to care about anything sitting on my head. My hands gripped her hips, and I felt the lacy lingerie against my fingertips. Her tits were getting bigger and bigger every day, and now they spilled over her bra. When she ground against me, I could feel the slit in her panties that led directly to her pussy.

I moaned.

She raised herself so she could slide down my length. Slowly, she moved until every inch of my dick was deep inside her—exactly where it belonged. She wiggled her hips and got comfortable on my lap, as if she was adjusting my dick to exactly where she wanted it to be. Her hands planted against my chest, and she slowly started to move up and down, her sexy belly moving with her.

Fuck, this was hot.

My hands cupped her stomach as I felt her lift herself up and drag down again. She sheathed me with all of her arousal, all of her cream. I felt it coat my dick everywhere, making me so slick and wet.

Her pussy was amazing.

She gripped my wrists for balance and tilted her head back, moaning as she enjoyed how hard I got for her. I knew she could feel my dick, feel how much it thickened just for her. She was the only woman who could get me this hard, who could make me so thick I might rip in half.

She kept her movements slow, taking her time as she enjoyed me. She did all the work, her pussy grabbing my dick and holding on with possession. Her green eyes were as beautiful as the ornaments downstairs, and they glowed with a special warmth. She tilted her body forward and arched her back differently, dragging her pussy down my length as her mouth moved to mine.

Fuck, I wanted to come so bad.

She was so wet for me.

Wetter than she'd ever been.

My hands palmed her tits, but that just made it worse. It made me want to come harder, come deeper.

She gripped my shoulders and rested her forehead against mine as her hips continued to do their magical work. "I love you…" Her nails dug into me as she confessed her deepest feelings.

Like last time, my cock twitched inside her, barely restraining itself. I did better than last time, but barely. It was such an erotic moment, and to top it off, this gorgeous woman confessed her love for me. She didn't care if I didn't say it back. Lost in the moment, the words slipped from her lips. Her passion took over, and her logic died away. She opened her legs and her heart to me, giving me everything she had.

"You're the only man I've ever loved. The only man I want to love as long as I live." She spoke the words against my mouth, her whispers so sultry and sexy.

Fuck, that was the hottest thing I'd ever heard. On my lap and nearly six months pregnant, she was so gorgeous. She wanted me so much, wanted me for me. She didn't want me to go to work and make more money. She wanted me to spend time with her, to get hot chocolate and just be together. "Baby…" I tried to restrain myself, but it was impossible. I was an asshole most hours of the day, but I was a gentleman in the sack. I always let a woman come first before I released. But for a second time, I couldn't. I couldn't fight the urge that started in my balls. With a moan, I released inside her, pumping her with my seed while the pleasure stimulated all of my nerves. Like the last time she'd said those words, my climax was good. So raw.

"I love the way your come feels inside me." Her fingers moved into my hair, and she kissed me softly on the mouth. "So heavy." She didn't make me feel like shit for coming so soon. It seemed to arouse her, to know her sexy words were the ultimate turn-on for me. "You're the only man I've ever felt like this..."

Instantly, she got me hard again. My cock had just released a load deep inside her, but he was ready again within a minute. With other women, I usually needed fifteen minutes before I wanted another round, and most of the time, I didn't even want to have sex again. I'd been sleeping with the same woman for months, and instead of getting tired of her, I craved her more. Even when I did get my fill of her, it was never truly enough.

"God, he's so hard again..." She started to bounce on me once more.

If she kept this up, I was going to blow my load too soon again. I rolled her onto her back and then ground between her legs, rubbing right against her clit. I needed to make her come before I slipped up again. "Baby." I held my face above her and watched her enjoy me. I moved hard and fast the second we began, wanting to drive her into the kind of climax that made her toes curl.

It didn't take long. She cupped my face as she moaned. "Cato...I love you. God, I love you."

Fuck. Just as I pushed her into an orgasm, she forced me to have another. I joined her in the climax, both of us moaning with pleasure. I gave her more come, and she took it deep. I kept thrusting until we were both completely finished, our bodies softening together.

She slid her hands up my chest then cupped my face. The look of love in her eyes said everything her lips didn't utter. Her soft fingertips stroked my jawline, and then she brought my mouth to hers for another kiss.

Even though we were both satisfied and I had an early morning tomorrow, I matched her kisses. I kissed her slowly, my mouth moving with hers like there was nothing else I'd rather be doing. Even if sex was off the table, this intimacy was more than enough. I could kiss her forever, enjoy her for a lifetime.

2

SIENA

I ordered Cato a holiday sweater online and got myself one too. Mine had Santas on it, and his had reindeer. I knew he would never want to wear something like that, so I would definitely have to talk him into it.

Giovanni watched me open everything at the kitchen counter. "I've got to be honest, Miss Siena. I don't think Mr. Marino is going to wear that."

"I'll have to talk him into it, I know."

"You've changed that man a lot, but I'm not sure if you can make miracles."

"You never know." I held up the sweater against my body. "Cute, huh?"

"Very."

"Once I talk him into this, I want you to take a picture of us in front of the tree."

Giovanni laughed like I'd made a joke. "Mr. Marino would fire me."

"He would not. Come on, please? It's his Christmas gift."

"Torturing him?"

"No, I'm making him something for Christmas. I think he'll like it." He liked my sonogram picture, so he should like this too. "But I need to get this picture first."

"Good luck with that, Miss Siena."

I folded up the boxes and placed them in the recycling bin. "What are your plans for Christmas?"

"I'll make Christmas dinner for Mr. Marino then see my children at their mother's house."

"He didn't give you the whole day off?" I asked incredulously. "It's Christmas."

"It's fine," he said, always smiling. "Mr. Marino doesn't know how to cook."

"But I do."

"You're pregnant, Miss Siena. You should rest."

"I'm not disabled. I can put a bird in the oven and make stuffing."

Giovanni dropped the subject. "It's interesting to think there will be a baby here this time next year."

"Yes...a little girl." I still had a long way to go, but I was very excited about getting my daughter at the end. "Martina Marino."

"Very cute name."

"Yes. Cato loves it." I rubbed my hand across my stomach. "You've known Cato for a long time. Anything interesting you can tell me about him?"

"I don't know him as well as I thought I did."

"What does that mean?"

"Well..." He finished placing the sugar cookies on the baking sheet before he carried them to the oven. They were cut out into candy canes, sleighs, and reindeer. He took off the oven mitts and returned to me. "If someone had asked me if Mr. Marino would settle down with a woman, I would have said no. If someone had asked me if Mr. Marino would have a family, I would have said no too. He's turned into a man I never thought I would meet. So, in the end...I think you know him better than I do."

I smiled. "He's turned into a big sweetheart, hasn't he?"

Giovanni shrugged. "He's not trying to hide it as much."

"Sometimes I wonder if we would be here right now if I weren't pregnant. But with our connection, I think it would have happened anyway. I think Cato took advantage of my pregnancy to spare my life...just so he had an excuse to do it."

Giovanni grabbed his alarm and set the timer for the cookies. "I think everything would have been exactly the same. Mr. Marino is a very paranoid man. The fact that he stopped wearing protection with anyone is an indicator of how he felt about you. He wouldn't have done that with anyone else. He's met the right woman, but I think he's still resisting the truth. He'll come around when he's ready."

"Yes...I just hope that's sooner rather than later." When we made love, I couldn't resist the urge to tell him how I felt. I couldn't hold back the passion, the love inside my heart. Even if he didn't say it back, I wanted to say it anyway. I wanted to share that moment with the special man I adored. He could deny how he felt about me, but every time I said it, he couldn't control his releases; it turned him on to hear those pretty words.

"He's a complicated man. I suspect it'll take a bit of time. I've seen the other women he's been with." He shook his head. "Maybe it was fun at the time, but they don't care about him at all. He could drop dead, and they would pick his pockets and steal whatever they could find. They pretend to be exactly what he wants in the hope they'll get a diamond ring and access to his wealth. You're the only woman I've met who seems to appreciate him for who he is...so he'd better not do something stupid and lose you."

Cato stepped through the door, dressed in his navy suit and black tie. Spots of water were on his clothes because it'd been raining all day. "Who better not do something stupid and lose you?" He joined me at the kitchen counter and wrapped his arm around my waist.

Giovanni was saved when the timer went off. "Better get the cookies..." He opened the oven and pulled out the tray.

Cato looked down at me, suspicion in his eyes.

"Giovanni said I'm the only woman who's ever liked you for you...and you'd be stupid to let me go." My fingers walked up his tie before I rose onto my tiptoes and kissed him on the mouth.

He kissed me back.

Giovanni set the tray of cookies on the counter. "They came out nice."

Cato broke our kiss and examined the cookies the two of us had made together. "What are these?"

"You can make billions of dollars but not figure out these are cookies?" I asked incredulously. I grabbed a candy cane and broke off a piece for him to try.

He pushed my hand away. "No thank you."

"You'll stay at six percent even with a bite." I pressed it against his lips again.

He finally ate out of my hand, his eyes locked to mine.

"Good. You need to live a little." I ate the other half of the candy cane. "Yum...those are amazing."

Even Giovanni ate one.

"I don't know how much I like the two of you spending all day together," Cato said. "Plotting against me..."

"We talk about you all the time," I said honestly. "But we don't plot against you. And no, we never say anything negative."

"Sure." Cato stripped off his jacket and hung it on the back of the chair. He pulled his tie off next.

"By the way, Giovanni is getting Christmas off," I said. "And I will make Christmas dinner."

Giovanni dropped the cookie dough he was scooping. "Sir, I didn't agree to that. I'm more than happy to make Christmas dinner. It's absolutely no trouble—"

"He's taking the day off. He gets to sleep in and spend the day with his kids. They'll both be home for the holidays." Giovanni worked seven days a week, and it was inhumane that he ever had to work on Christmas. "I'll make dinner. You've had my cooking. You know it's good."

Cato stared at me coldly, like he didn't approve of that at all. "I'm the master of this house, not you. If I want to give my employees a day off, I will. You don't call the shots around here. I do."

My eyebrow rose so high at the cold way he'd just spoken to me. Everything eventually came back to his ego, his need for power. If I ever crossed the line, he always put me in my place. "You tell me to make myself at home here, and then the second I do, you act like an asshole again. You say you want to take care of me, but then I do something nice for your most loyal employee and offer to cook for your family, and that somehow offends you? Take your ego and shove it up your ass, Cato. If I didn't love you so much, I would shove my foot up your ass myself." I stormed off and left the Christmas sweaters behind.

Cato came up behind me and grabbed me by the elbow. "Baby, hold on."

I twisted out of his grasp. "Don't *baby* me."

He grabbed me again. "I'm sorry, alright? I don't know why I do that sometimes."

I turned back to him. "Because you're an egotistical asshole. Is this my home too? Or am I still a guest here? Because I thought after everything we've been through, having a baby together, being in love with each other, that I would have more rights than what you're giving me. I signed that paperwork excluding me from ever getting a dime from you. If that's not the ultimate declaration of love, then what is?"

For the first time, Cato was speechless. He stared at me with a pained expression, like he wished he had something good to say.

"I just wanted to do something nice for Giovanni. Didn't realize that was so fucking terrible." I marched out the door and left him behind, wanting him to think about his behavior and know that I wouldn't put up with it. Not now. Not ever.

———

Thirty minutes later, he came upstairs.

I sat on the couch and watched TV, expecting to ignore him for the rest of the night. He would probably apologize and we would have make-up sex, but for right now, I was still pissed. We'd been having such a good week, spending time in front of the fire talking, decorating the Christmas tree, and making love in Christmas lingerie. Just when things got really good, he fucked them up. It was like he sabotaged himself on purpose.

He stepped inside the doorway. "Baby?"

I kept my eyes on the TV and didn't look at him. "I'm not done ignoring you."

He moved into the room then stood in front of the TV, blocking the screen and forcing me to look at him.

That was when I noticed the Christmas sweater. The reindeer pattern covered the green sweater, all of them with red noses. It fit him perfectly, but it also looked comical because it was something he would never, ever wear.

My mouth dropped open.

"Giovanni encouraged me to put this on. Said it might help you forgive me."

I still couldn't believe he was wearing it. And I couldn't believe how handsome he looked either. The guy could literally wear anything and still look like the sexiest man in the world. "You have to apologize first."

"I did—"

"Then do it again."

In his hand was my sweater. He tossed it on the couch beside me and slid his hands into the pockets of his jeans. "I know I acted like an asshole. I'm sorry."

"And?"

"And what? What else do you want me to say?"

"Why did you act like that in the first place? The week has been magical, and then you switch on me."

He shifted his gaze to the floor as he considered his answer. He pressed his lips tightly together, his jaw clenching as that big brain of his worked. He pulled his left hand out of his pocket then ran it through his hair. "I think that was the problem."

My eyes softened.

"I never wanted this. Now it feels like I've got a wife and a kid..."

"But you're happy—"

"I'm really fucking happy." His powerful voice came out strong, filling the air with his innate power. "Doesn't alter the fact that everything's changing. I'm not the man with you as the prisoner. Now, I feel like the damn prisoner. I can't escape your beauty, the way you make me feel, and I can't stop thinking about you all day at work. On top of that, I never wanted a family, and now I'm having a daughter...and I fucking love her more than anything. It's like... my heart lives outside my body. Everything has changed so drastically, and I fucking hate it." He moved his hand back into his hand and looked at me.

Hot tears burned under my eyes, but I didn't let them fall. I couldn't care less that he wouldn't say he loved me. He'd just admitted it in his own way.

"I don't care if Giovanni works or not. I don't care if you want to make Christmas dinner. I couldn't care less. It just reminded me that I don't have as much power anymore... because I'm sharing it with you."

I hated it when he acted like an asshole, but when he poured his heart out to me, it made me love him even more than I did before. My heart began to love him even more deeply. "Is sharing power that difficult?"

He continued to stand in front of the TV. "My father made all the money. Mother didn't work. So when he took off, we were penniless. Mother had to work two jobs, and by the time I was fourteen, I was picking up work wherever I could. My mother didn't have any skills because she assumed she would be a housewife. Watching my father abandon us haunted me, but being so dependent on him was the worst part. None of us were prepared for it. I just never want to feel that way again, to rely on someone to be there and then they leave me destitute."

I stared at the strong man I'd fallen in love with, and I knew his boyish roots were still deep in his soul. He was the strongest man I knew, a powerful provider and a ruthless dictator. But his ambitions were ruled by heartbreak. "I'm not going anywhere, Cato."

"You left me once."

"Because I—"

"You took my daughter away from me. You took you away from me."

"Let's not forget why," I said gently, not wanting him to flip the story on me.

He turned his gaze and looked out the window. "I just don't like someone having more power than me—in any scenario. I need to control everything, even something so minor as the staff. You aren't a guest here. But this is still my domain."

I could tell he was continuing to keep me at a distance, but I couldn't understand why. There was always a subtle wall keeping us apart. I didn't know if he still contemplated killing me. Or maybe his feelings didn't mirror mine. "Is that why you won't tell me you love me?" Confessing feelings as strong as those would give me the upper hand. I would know how he really felt—and I could use that to my advantage.

He didn't give me an answer. "I'm sorry for the way I acted. But that's just how I am. I can't promise it won't happen again in the future. That would require me to be a different person."

"People turn into different people all the time. It's called growing. Whether you like it or not, you're growing every day. You're slowly becoming a different man—a better man. I know it'll take time for you to trust me fully, and

I've got all the time in the world. Regardless of your dumb outbursts, I'll still love you. I may yell at you and slap you upside the head, but my love will never change. I'll never abandon you, Cato. As long as you never give me a reason to."

His blue eyes turned to mine, and there was a slight hint of emotion in his gaze. He was still boarded up like an old house that was almost too much work to fix. But with enough care and patience, he could be better than he ever was. "Why did you want me to wear this?"

I stood up and pulled on mine. "You'll see."

He shook his head slightly. "I don't think I want to see."

"You owe me, alright? Don't forget it."

"Like you would ever let me."

We headed downstairs and stood in front of the tree. "Giovanni?"

He came out of the kitchen and tried not to laugh when he looked at Cato.

"If you want to keep your job, I suggest you keep it together," Cato warned.

I nudged him in the side. "Don't talk like that." I handed Giovanni the phone.

Giovanni held it up then indicated for us to squeeze together.

Cato realized what was happening. "You've got to be kidding me…"

"You're still in the doghouse, remember?"

"Who's gonna see this?" he demanded. "I can't let—"

"No one is going to see this, I promise. It's for me. And even if it weren't, you still have some making up to do. So just smile."

Cato finally cooperated. He stood slightly behind me with his hands on my stomach. I rested mine over his. Giovanni got a few shots then handed the phone back.

"These look great," I said as I scrolled through.

"Good." Cato took off the sweater right away, standing in nothing but his jeans. "Don't expect me to wear this again."

————

I washed off my makeup and lay beside him in bed. I was in one of his baggy t-shirts, and I turned off my lamp on my bedside table. Once the room was covered in darkness, I closed my eyes.

Cato moved to my side of the bed and pressed his chest against my back. "I apologized."

"So?"

"You are going to keeping torturing me for nothing?"

"Just want to make sure you learned your lesson."

His hard cock was pressed against me, right between my cheeks. He ground against me, his lips resting against my ear. "Baby, come on."

"Nope. Go to sleep."

"You really think I'm going to just go to sleep with a babe like you beside me?"

The compliment tempted me, but I still didn't move.

"If you're going to sleep with me every night, you have to pay your dues."

"Oh, really?" I countered. "So now I owe you something?"

"We owe each other something. So, give it up, or sleep down the hall."

"I'm the one who's pissed at you, remember?"

He grabbed my hip and slowly rolled me onto my back. "Then be pissed at me while I fuck you."

"You're such an asshole—" The words died in my mouth when I felt his big cock inside me.

He locked his arms behind my knees and fucked me hard. "I know I am. But fuck me anyway." His lips moved to mine, and he gave me a hard kiss.

The second we thrust together, I abandoned my need for distance. I wanted to torture him for a bit, but once I felt him inside me, I couldn't. I melted like a stick of butter in a hot pan. "Cato…"

"Baby." He rested his face against my cheek. "I thought about this pussy all day. I always think about this pussy all day."

"What about me? Do you ever think about me?"

"Yes," he said as he thrust. "Always."

3

CATO

It was a few days before Christmas. Florence was busier than usual as everyone finished their last-minute Christmas shopping. There was a lot of new business for the company this time of year. Lots of companies were looking for tax shelters before the end of the year. As a result, they dumped it into my investments—which made me money.

The administrative offices would be closed through the new year. Bates and I were usually back at the office the day after Christmas, but this year, I thought I might stay home and enjoy myself a bit.

It would make Siena and my mother happy.

Bates walked into my office. "You busy?"

"Always." It'd been a better working environment since that deep talk we'd had. Now Bates wasn't so hostile all the time. He was my friend again.

He sat in the chair anyway and then tossed me a cigar.

I needed to stop smoking so much, but the second he handed me one, I couldn't resist. "What?"

"I've been trying to get some intel on Micah and Damien. Nothing. No one knows what they're up to. No one knows what their business is doing. They've gone underground and haven't made any movements."

"What's interesting about that?" I'd granted them mercy because I'd needed something from them. They got lucky —really lucky. "They narrowly escaped annihilation. They probably want to stay off my radar."

"I think it's suspicious. No one is that quiet. They have absolutely no business dealings. Their drug trade has completely stopped. If they aren't selling drugs, then what the hell are they doing?"

"Maybe they're getting out of the game." After publicly challenging me, they may have found it too difficult to continue business when they looked like pussies.

"No one gets out of the game. No such thing."

Siena would be thrilled if I got out of the game. "There's no way to know what happened. Speculating isn't going to give you answers."

"I just think we need to be on alert."

"You really think they would challenge us after I granted them a truce?"

He shrugged. "Maybe they think you're weak now."

"Or they are beneath me and not worth my time."

"Or you're so deep in pussy you aren't thinking clearly."

My eyes narrowed.

"I'm not taking a shot at Siena." He held up both of his hands. "I'm just saying, they may know about your infatuation with her and want to take advantage of it. I've seen headlines in the media that you're expecting."

That only took a few days to circulate. My brother never paid attention to that stuff, so if he knew about it, so did everyone else.

"And knocking up a woman is pretty difficult these days, considering all the shit you can use to prevent it." He gave me an accusatory look. "A condom, for instance. Birth control..."

"She was on birth control."

"Or was she…?"

"She was." I believed her. She had no reason to lie. "And I don't regret what happened, so it doesn't matter. Seeing her get bigger every month just makes me look forward to meeting my daughter."

Bates stopped giving me a hard time about it. "I think there's something going on right under our noses."

"And what are we supposed to do about that?"

"Storm their headquarters."

"Even though we're under a truce? That'll make me look like a liar. That's the last thing I need."

"Looking like a liar is better than looking like a fool. We could at least stop by and see what they're up to. You know, scare them a little bit."

"How would you respond if Damien stopped by our office just to see what we're doing?"

Bates's gaze darkened.

"They'd probably shoot us. I get you're paranoid, but a lack of activity doesn't mean they're plotting anything against us. And even if they are, they've got way fewer men than we do. Way fewer assets. Way fewer allies."

"And now they know what we're capable of, so they'll be better prepared. The fact that you granted them a truce just shows you underestimate them. If they realize that, it'll make them even more likely to attack."

When my brother set his mind on something, he didn't change it. Sometimes he was right; sometimes he was wrong. This time, he just seemed paranoid. "I think we should let this go until we have concrete information. Stating that business is slow isn't a good enough reason to assume war is on the horizon."

"Let's not forget that they foolishly tried to get a woman to take you in. They want you for something, Cato. I would have been an easier target, but they still went after you. Why?"

I didn't have a clue. "I don't know, man."

"I feel it in my gut, Cato. Something isn't right. I can't explain it, I can't give any facts. But I just know there's something going on right under our noses. These guys aren't big enough to replace us, but they definitely want something. Anyone who could overthrow us and access our accounts could shortcut their way to the top of the food chain."

"But they would need both of us. Just taking me down wouldn't accomplish anything."

"Unless I was forced to surrender everything to save you."

We'd talked about this eventuality in the past. It wasn't a topic we discussed often because it was too painful. "You know you can't do that. I'd rather die than let our enemies take what we've built." Siena would be disappointed in me for saying that, that I would die for money. But it was more than money to me. It was pride in everything I'd achieved.

He nodded in understanding. "Keep your eyes peeled. Make sure Siena doesn't leave the house. Their behavior may have something to do with her."

Damien would never get close to Siena ever again. I wouldn't shoot his other shoulder if he did. I'd shoot him right in the head this time. "Coming over for Christmas?"

"You know I have no other plans, except with the whore I bought myself."

The corner of my mouth lifted in a smile because I knew he wasn't joking. "You get tired of that?"

"Not yet. You get tired of fucking a pregnant woman?"

"Not in the slightest."

He made a disgusted face. "I'm not into that shit."

"If you get a woman pregnant, you'll understand."

"I'm not dumb enough to do that. I always wear a rubber—even when the woman begs me not to."

"If you found a good woman, you wouldn't have to. And trust me...there's nothing like it. I could never go back."

"What does that mean?" he asked. "You could never be with another woman besides Siena?"

"No. I just couldn't wear a condom again."

He took a big puff on the cigar. "That sounds like the same thing to me."

"It's not."

"Is it?" He left the white smoke drift from his mouth. "You're so pussy-whipped, I can't picture you with someone else. If that's how you feel, then fine. I just figured you would have the balls to own up to it."

I rolled the cigar between my fingertips. "I feel like all we ever talk about is what I'm doing with my dick."

"I just told you what I'm doing with my dick on Christmas. And she's the most expensive hooker I've ever paid for."

"Bates, you don't need to pay for a hooker. You can get whatever you want."

He was about to smoke his cigar again, but he lowered it. "Did you just give me a compliment?"

"Just stating the obvious. You're handsome and a rich guy. You don't need to pay for sex."

"You've paid for sex."

"That's just for the really kinky shit."

"I like kinky shit too." He put his cigar in his mouth. "So, can I bring the hooker with me to dinner?"

I glared at him. "You think Mother would like that?"

He shrugged. "You're her favorite, so what does it matter?"

"No. Siena isn't going to want to cook for a hooker."

"Whoa, hold on." He dropped the cigar into the ashtray and knocked off all the ash. "What happened to Giovanni?"

"Siena gave him the day off."

"Uh, who does she think she is? What the hell are we gonna eat? Giovanni is the best."

I shrugged. "She said she can cook."

"What? Mac and cheese?"

I kept smoking my cigar. "She's cooked for me a few times, actually. She's good."

"But it's Christmas. She's ruining tradition."

"It's what she wanted. Giovanni has worked every Christmas since I can remember. Giving him the day off isn't ridiculous."

"But he could make the food in the morning and then leave. We can pop that shit in the microwave."

"Bates, it'll be fine. You don't even care about Christmas."

"I care about the food," he snapped.

"You have your own chef."

"But she's no Giovanni. If you ever fire him, I'm taking him."

"Well, I'm never going to fire him," I countered.

"You fired him on Christmas..."

"Siena did. I didn't."

"Does she run the house?" Bates finished his cigar and left the remains in the ashtray.

"Don't start with me, Bates. We just started getting along."

He rolled his eyes. "Whatever. I just don't like it when someone fucks up our traditions."

"You haven't tried her cooking. Maybe it'll be better."

"Yeah...better than Giovanni's," he said sarcastically. "Sure..."

———

It was the first time I'd woken up on Christmas morning with a woman beside me.

A beautiful, pregnant woman.

Her hair was all over my shoulder, and her body was tangled with mine. The heater kept the house at the optimal temperature, but she still sucked the heat from my body like she was freezing.

I opened my eyes and stared at her for a while.

Her hand moved to her stomach, and she opened her eyes as she felt the baby kick. "She's awake..."

"Because it's Christmas." My hand moved over her belly. Her stomach wasn't really that big, but she was so petite that she looked enormous right off the bat. "Or she's just hungry."

She chuckled. "Maybe it's that." She moved her hand over my chest as she snuggled closer to me. "Merry Christmas."

I brushed my lips across her hairline. "Merry Christmas, baby."

"Let's go downstairs and open presents and have some breakfast."

"What about sex?"

She chuckled. "Can we have sex later?"

"Why?" My favorite thing about waking up in the morning when I didn't have to go to work was sex. I wasn't in a hurry, so I could take my time, really enjoy that cunt that made me a better man.

"Alright. How do you want it?"

"The same way I always want it." I moved on top of her and settled between her thighs. My cock found her slick entrance, and I moved inside like a jetliner landing on a runway—completely smooth.

She locked her ankles together at my lower back and gripped the backs of my shoulders. "Yes..."

———

When we went into the kitchen, Giovanni had breakfast on the counter, the plates covered with foil. There was also a note.

Sorry, Mr. Marino. Couldn't resist.

-Gio

She tore off the foil and eyed the scrambled eggs, bacon, and waffles. "Now that's what I call a breakfast." She grabbed a strip of bacon and took a bite out of it, the crunch audible between her teeth. "It's so good, I'm not even mad."

I didn't eat shit like this for breakfast, but since it was Christmas, I made an exception. I grabbed a strip of bacon and ate it. "Not bad."

Siena made me a cup of coffee, and we sat together at the counter and ate our breakfast.

I sipped my coffee while I looked at her, wearing my sweatpants and one of her tank tops. She had to roll the top of the pants twenty times so they wouldn't drag across the floor, but she somehow made it look cute anyway.

"I got a gift for you." She tore a piece of her waffle and dunked it in the syrup.

"You did?"

"Yep."

"Hope it's slutty."

She rolled her eyes. "It's not."

"Then I don't want it."

She smacked my arm playfully. "Shut up. That's not the only thing you care about, and you know it." She carried our dishes to the sink before she returned to me. "Let's open gifts. I have to start cooking soon."

"Really? It's ten in the morning."

"The turkey takes a long time."

"You know there's only four of us, right?" Unless my brother really did bring that hooker.

"Still takes a long time." She walked up to the tree then grabbed the small gift bag from the ground. She placed it in my hands. "It's not much, but I think you'll like it."

I still didn't like getting gifts, but since it was Siena, I didn't complain. I pulled the tissue out of the bag then grabbed something by a string of ribbon. It was Christmas ornament, but it was customized with the picture we took the other day. We were standing together and showing off her pregnant belly, both wearing those ridiculous Christmas sweaters. The date was written at the top along with a message. "Can't wait to meet you, Martina." I held the ornament in my hand as I stared at the image for a long time, seeing all of her emotions wrapped up into a single gift. It was thoughtful, personal, and couldn't have cost her more than five dollars. It was perfect. "Thank you." I lifted my gaze and met hers.

"Do you like it?"

"I do." I found an unencumbered branch and hung it at eye level. "I got you something too."

"Let me guess? It's slutty."

I grabbed the box from under the tree and handed it to her. "No, unfortunately. But you can put on that little red number you showed me last week."

"You'd want me to wear that again?"

"Wear it every night, especially with that Santa hat."

She took the small box and ripped off the wrapping paper. What was left behind was a small teal box with a bow on top. The name of the jewelry designer was written across the surface. Instead of taking off the lid, she looked up at me. "Cato, you know I don't want anything expensive—"

"Just open it."

She sighed then removed the lid. Inside was a white-gold bracelet with three charms attached. Each charm had a different initial. S. C. M. It was the first initial of each of our names. She looked at each one, and then understanding slowly started to creep in.

"I wasn't going to get you something cheap out of principle. I want you to have something that will last forever."

She took the bracelet out of the box and rubbed each charm with her fingers. "I love it, Cato. So sweet…" When she looked up at me, there were tears in her eyes. "Thank you so much." She moved into my chest and hugged me.

My arms encircled her petite frame, and I squeezed her tight. She was at the ideal height so I could rest my chin on her head. Both of our gifts had been perfect for each other —and they both centered around the little girl we were having.

She pulled away then extended her wrist. "Could you help me?"

I put it around her slender wrist then clasped it into place.

She admired the way it looked around her wrist, the way the charms shifted along the metal. "Perfect." She rose onto her tiptoes and kissed me. "It's not slutty, but I still love it."

I chuckled. "If you wore nothing but that bracelet, that might work."

"Not a bad idea..."

4

SIENA

I was working hard in the kitchen, trying to keep everything warm while I prepared the next part of the meal. The turkey was almost done, the stuffing was covered in foil, the potatoes would have to be reheated, and the other sides needed to pop in the microwave for a few minutes each.

"Need help, baby?" Cato walked into the kitchen, looking undeniably sexy in his long-sleeved maroon shirt and black jeans. He'd looked better naked a few hours ago, but after a shower and a shave, he'd cleaned up real nice.

"No. Almost done."

The doorbell rang.

"That must be them. Bates picked up my mother on the way."

"Okay, great." I washed my hands and untied my apron.

Cato opened the front door and greeted them both. "Mother, you look nice." He hugged her and kissed her on the cheek. "Merry Christmas."

"Merry Christmas, honey." She gave her son an affectionate look, like he was the apple of her eye. She moved to me next and gave me the same excited expression. "Merry Christmas, Siena. You look stunning." She touched my belly before she hugged me. "You're glowing brighter than..." She pointed at the tree. "There's a tree up?"

"I had to fight Cato for a bit, but I eventually won."

"It's beautiful," she said. "Perfect for this space."

Cato greeted his brother. "Merry Christmas."

"Yeah, whatever." Bates handed him a present. "Got you something. Don't care if you don't like it."

He chuckled. "Merry Christmas to you too."

We gathered in the dining room.

"Mother, what can I get for you to drink? White wine?"

"Sure," she said as she took off her gloves.

"I'll have scotch," Bates said.

"Two wines, it is." Cato poured two glasses and handed them over.

I was just about to head into the kitchen when the door-bell rang again. I opened the door and came face-to-face with Landon. "Hey. So glad you could make it." I hugged him and welcomed him inside.

"I won't turn down a home-cooked meal—even if you may have poisoned it." He smiled as he stepped inside.

I escorted him into the other room and introduced him to everyone. Then I put my apron back on. "Everything is just about ready."

Chiara looked at me with an appalled look. "Are you cooking?"

"Yep," Bates said. "They gave Giovanni the day off."

"Do you need any help, dear?" Chiara asked. "A pregnant woman should be relaxing."

"I'm fine," I said with a laugh. "I'm not disabled. But you can carry the stuffing to the table. Bates, could you put these sides in the microwave for two minutes each? And Cato, could you carve the turkey?"

Cato opened the door to the oven. "Sure, baby." He carried it to the counter and started to slice the meat.

Chiara stared at her son with a knowing look, but he was too focused to catch it.

The five of us worked together to get everything on the table. We gathered around, and Chiara made a toast. She held up her glass. "I'm very lucky to have two incredible sons who take such good care of me. Soon, I'll have a granddaughter, and hopefully more grandchildren to add to the family." She turned to me. "And I'm grateful to have Siena in our lives, to make my son into a good man and fill this home with happiness. There's a tree in the entryway, the staff got the day off, and you prepared this beautiful meal. You're a wonderful woman. And to Landon, Siena's brother, we're all family here." She raised her glass and tapped it against mine. "Merry Christmas."

"Merry Christmas." The rest of us did the same.

Cato stared at his mother for a while but didn't say anything. He seemed annoyed with her words rather than pleased.

But maybe I was reading too much into it.

———

After dinner, gifts were exchanged. Bates handed Cato the present he'd brought in earlier. "Open it." He practically tossed it at him.

Cato ripped open the box and found a blue watch inside. He turned it over and saw the engraving in the metal on the back. "To my big brother. Merry Xmas."

I smiled, touched by the gesture Bates had made.

Cato patted his brother on the shoulder. "Thanks, man. I love it."

"I got you these too." He pulled out a box of Cubans. "Best of the best."

Cato took off the watch he was wearing and put his brother's on instead. "It's a good fit. And thanks for the cigars."

I'd noticed Cato smelled like smoke from time to time, but I didn't realize he smoked on a daily basis. It was something I would have to ask him about later. The father of my child wasn't going to die ten years too soon because of a disgusting habit.

"What did you get me?" Bates asked, extending his hand.

"I'll go get it." He walked to the tree, grabbed the gift, and returned.

I thought it was interesting that the two men argued most of the time, but they put their disagreements to the side and showed each other love—in discreet ways. I'd also noticed that Bates wasn't nearly as vicious to me as he usually was. He was actually pleasant. Maybe that was because their mother was right there.

Cato handed it over. "I think you'll like it."

Bates ripped off the wrapping then admired the remote-control helicopter. It looked like a child's toy, and when Bates's face lit up, he looked like a child meeting Santa Claus. "This thing looks sick."

"It has a pretty good radius too," Cato said. "I've got some batteries in the drawer."

"Awesome," Bates said. "Can't wait to fly this thing. Thanks, man."

Chiara smiled as she watched her two sons. "They're so ornery sometimes, but they show their love when it matters most." She turned to me, and her eyes focused on my bracelet. "That's beautiful. What do these letters mean?"

"Cato got it for me," I explained. "C is his initial. S is mine. And M is for Martina."

"Is that what you decided to name her?" she asked with a smile. "That's an adorable name."

"Thank you. He gave the bracelet to me this morning."

"That was so thoughtful." She gave Cato a look full of consideration. "Very thoughtful."

Cato drank his wine in response.

I moved my wrist to Landon so he could admire it.

He didn't care about things like that, but he was polite enough to give me a compliment. "Nice."

After we finished drinking and spending the evening together, the men cleaned up. Landon did the dishes while Cato and Bates packed up the leftover food and made room in the fridge. Bates grabbed a plastic container and opened the lid. "Dump some turkey and stuffing in here. Oh, and some potatoes. I'll even take that asparagus."

Cato shoveled the food into the container with a grin on his face. "You liked my woman's cooking, huh?"

Bates made a sour face.

"Guess you don't miss Giovanni that much." Cato scooped the potatoes into another container.

Chiara watched them for a moment before she turned back to me. She lowered her voice so they couldn't over-hear us. "You did a great job tonight. The food was wonderful. You're an excellent cook."

"Thank you."

"And you'll be an excellent mother."

That compliment meant a lot more. "Thank you."

She held my gaze with the same intensity her oldest son sometimes showed. "My son loves you, Siena. Very much." She patted my hand on the table. "I'm very happy he has such good taste. I'm not oblivious to all the things my son does in his private life. But I'm relieved he didn't want that to continue for the rest of his life. When he found a good woman, he recognized it."

I'd always heard getting the approval of a man's mother was no easy task. Especially with Chiara, I'd thought she would be more protective because all she had were her sons. But earning her approval was a million times easier than earning Cato's. "I love him with all my heart." I wasn't ashamed to say those words out loud, not when my feelings were written across the surface of my eyes. I told Cato how I felt often, regardless of his silence.

His mother smiled. "I already knew that. I can tell just by looking at you. My son told me on several occasions that he doesn't love you, that there's no future here. I'm glad he was wrong."

"Well...he hasn't actually told me he loves me."

"Really?" she asked, the disappointment filling her gaze. "But you know he does, right?"

"Yes." My hand rested on my stomach. "I do. He's just not ready to say it. And that's fine...because I've got all the time in the world."

She rubbed my arm gently. "He's worth the wait, I promise you. Cato may have a rough exterior, but he's got such a big heart underneath all that macho bullshit. The second he had some money in his wallet, he came to my job and forced me to quit that day. I was still in the cannery at the time. He told me he never wanted me to work again."

Emotion flooded my veins when I listened to the story. Cato was loyal and loving.

"I know he hates his father for abandoning me, for forcing me to provide for two boys when I'd never worked a day in my life. He wanted to take his father's place as the man of the house. I've always known he was trying to prove something to himself, that he's not like his father."

"He's a good man...and he's nothing like that coward."

"I could go on and on about my son's many qualities...but I'm sure you already know he's amazing. You never have to worry about a thing with him. He'll always take care of you, in every way you can imagine."

———

We said goodbye at the door.

To my astonishment, Bates actually gave me a compliment. "Dinner was great. Thanks for doing that." He held up his container of leftovers. "I'll eat this later tonight."

I couldn't wipe off the smirk on my face. "Are you just being nice because it's Christmas? Because if so, I wish it were Christmas every day."

"No," he said with a chuckle. "Cato showed me the paperwork you signed...so I guess you aren't a gold digger like I thought you were."

"No. I love your brother for who he is...even when he's being an asshole."

"Which is pretty often," he jabbed. "Well, goodnight." He said goodbye to his brother and stepped out into the cold.

Chiara hugged me. "Thank you again. Hope to see both of you soon." She kissed me on the cheek then embrace Cato. "I love you."

He held her close. "Love you too."

"Life is so short." She pulled away and gave him a smile. "You should always tell the people you love that you love them...because you might miss your chance." After giving him a knowing look, she walked out.

Landon said goodbye next. "Thanks for having me over. This is the nicest Christmas I've had since Mom died. Was she the one who taught you how to cook?"

"Yes, actually."

"Good. It felt like she was here tonight." He hugged me then kissed me on the forehead. "I'll see you later." He moved to Cato next and shook his hand. "Thanks for having me over. Merry Christmas."

"Merry Christmas." Cato watched him walk out before he shut the door behind him. The cold breeze disappeared, and the warmth surrounded us once more.

"Your brother was actually nice to me. Christmas miracles do exist."

"I think anytime food is involved, Bates is generally more tolerable."

"Then I need to have food out at all times."

"Not a bad idea." He walked with me back to the dining room, and we cleaned off the table together and rinsed the remaining glasses. The dishwasher was full, so we decided to leave the rest in the sink. When Giovanni returned tomorrow, he could take care of it.

"So, what did you and my mother talk about?" Cato asked as we headed upstairs to bed.

"A little of this, a little of that…"

"Why don't I believe you?"

"Because you're smarter than that." I walked through the door then undressed. My clothes smelled like Christmas food, mainly turkey and stuffing. The smell was in my hair too, but I was too tired to take a shower.

Cato stripped down to nothing, presumptuous about what would happen now that the night was over.

"I'm so tired, Cato. I cooked all day, my back is killing me, and I smell like a turkey."

He came up behind me and rubbed my shoulders. "Good thing I like the smell of turkey."

"Over lunch..." I closed my eyes and felt his fingers dig deep into muscles, working away at the tension and the fatigue.

"No. I like it when my woman smells like turkey...because she's been cooking for me all day." He guided me to the bed and onto my side so he could continue massaging my back. His fingers worked the muscles over my shoulder blades and those that hugged my spine. Whenever he found a knot, he slowly flattened it with his fingertips.

I was about to fall asleep. "If this is your way of getting sex...you're just putting me to sleep."

"If I wanted sex, I would just fuck you." His hand moved to my ass cheek, and he massaged that too.

"You're really good at that..."

His hands suddenly stopped moving. "What did you and my mother talk about?"

I opened my eyes and stared at the opposite wall. "You're evil."

"Tell me and I'll keep going."

He was giving me the best massage of my life, and I didn't want it to stop. "I told her I loved you."

He didn't rub my back. He stayed absolutely still, turning into a gargoyle. "And what did she say?"

"She said you loved me too. I told her you hadn't actually said the words but it was obvious. She agreed. That was about it. She told me you were a good man. She even told me about the day you went into the cannery and forced her to quit so you could take care of her. Not that she needed to give me another reason to love you."

He didn't massage my back again. His fingertips rested against my skin, the warmth entering my body and chasing away the cold from the open doorway. He didn't have a response to what I said, so he started to massage me again.

After minutes of silence, I drifted off to sleep.

5

CATO

Winter slowly turned to spring, and now that Siena was well into her eighth month, she became more uncomfortable—and more stressed.

"We don't have a crib, a car seat, diapers—nothing." 'She marched around our bedroom with her hand on her enormous stomach. "Which bedroom is going to be hers? We don't even know that. We're so unprepared."

"Baby—"

"We need to get this stuff now. Because I could pop at any moment."

"We still have at least another month."

"But babies come early all the time. We need to do this now."

"I have work."

She flashed me a look more terrifying than Satan's.

"I could have someone else take care of all that for us—"

"I don't want someone else to take care of this stuff for us." She stomped her foot. "I want to do all of it. I want to pick out her crib, find the perfect toys, buy an obscene number of diapers. It's a once-in-a-lifetime experience. It's our first child."

That made it sound like there would be more to follow. "Alright." I had an important meeting today, but Bates could take care of it. Siena was becoming more irrational with every passing day, probably because she was in pain most of the time. Her petite frame made carrying a child strenuous. "We'll take care of it today."

She finally relaxed once she got her way. "Let me change and we'll go."

I stepped into the hallway and called my brother.

"Where are you?" he barked. "You should have been here fifteen minutes ago."

"I can't come in today. I need you to handle this."

"Are you kidding me right now? This is a huge deal for us. Your balls better be stuck in the vacuum or something."

"I have other priorities I have to take care of right now."

His silence was a sharp indication of his rage. "The only other priority you have is Siena—and that's not a priority. You'll see her after work."

"We need to get stuff for Martina. She's having a meltdown about it."

"Do it after work."

"Bates, I've worked for our company day and night for the last decade. I've worked weekends and nights. I've lived for our company. But right now, this is more important. I'm going to be a father, and everything is going to change. When you have a kid, you'll understand. And I'll handle the office then so you can address it."

He sighed into the phone. "I'm never having a kid, so we don't need to worry about that."

"Whatever. I need to do this. I know you can handle it." I hung up before he could rip into me again.

———

We sat in the back seat of the car and headed to Florence where we would do our shopping. We were buying everything we might possibly need, and we had a separate car that would hold all our things.

I wore my black leather jacket with a green shirt underneath. Spring had arrived, but it was still cold as winter overshadowed the new season.

Siena was cozy in her jeans, an olive jacket with a fur hood, and a blue scarf. Tan boots were on her feet. Her distended belly was enormous now, and she constantly rubbed it like she could feel Martina move deep inside. She sighed every so often, like she was breathing through the distress.

There was nothing I could do for her at this point. No amount of back rubs or foot rubs would take away the discomfort she felt every single moment. She peed several times during the night and had morning sickness when she first woke up. Sex had become less appealing to her.

Which sucked for me.

I grabbed her hand and held it on my thigh, doing the only thing I possibly could in that moment. Affection was all I had to offer.

She rested her head against the back of the seat and sighed. "I loved being pregnant through most of this. But now I just can't wait for her to come out."

"You've done a great job, baby. You made it look easy."

"Liar." She smiled at me. "But thanks for saying it anyway."

My phone vibrated in my pocket, so I reached for it to check the message. I grabbed my pack of cigars by mistake and put them back before I retrieved my phone. It was a message from Bates, a quick question about the numbers. He should be in the meeting right now, so he probably hoped for a fast response. I typed back my answer right away.

Siena lifted her head and stared at my pocket. "Cato, do you smoke a lot?"

"No, not a lot."

"When do you smoke?"

"Mainly at work. Sometimes in my office."

"Well, you can't do that anymore."

No one ever told me what to do, so I gave her an incredulous look. "I don't smoke around you, and I always give my suit to Giovanni the second I get home. I'm not exposing you to it."

"That's not why, and you know it." She shot me that fierce expression, a warning of a bloody war. "Martina needs you to live as long as possible. Smoking cuts down your life expectancy by ten years. I understand why that wasn't important to you a year ago, but things are different now."

"I don't smoke cigarettes. I only smoke cigars for—"

"A cigar is the equivalent of seven cigarettes. Don't try to fool me, Cato. You aren't as smart as you think you are."

We hadn't had a fight like this in a long time. The last few months had been spent in comfort. Like most couples, we had a routine. I went to work, came home, we had dinner, and then we went to bed and had sex. It sounded boring, but it was actually very comfortable. It was a lot more fulfilling then heading to the bars and clubs like I used to.

"Promise me you'll never smoke again."

"For the rest of my life?" I asked incredulously.

"Yep."

"I only smoke once a week—"

"If you smoke so little, then it should be no problem to stop altogether." Blood lust was in her eyes, the same expression I wore when I manipulated my clients into agreeing to my outrageous terms. She wouldn't settle or negotiate. She made her demands, and I could meet them —or face the consequences.

"Baby, I appreciate what you're trying to do—"

"Cigars or sex. Pick."

Did she just give me an ultimatum? "You're being—"

"I'm serious, Cato. I love you too much to watch you slowly kill yourself. Smoking is the number one cause of premature death in the world."

When she tossed her love for me into the mix, I was blind-sided. She hadn't mentioned her feelings for me in several months, and then she dropped them when I least expected it. It always made me lose my footing. It made me feel good and terrible at the exact same time.

"No more." She snatched the cigars out of my pocket and threw them on the floor. "Promise me." She stared into my face until she heard the words she desired. She knew I wasn't the kind of man to make a promise I couldn't keep, so my word was good enough.

If she were someone else, I wouldn't comply out of princi-ple. If we weren't having a daughter in a month, I probably wouldn't care about giving her what she wanted. But I wanted to be around as long as possible so I could always take care of Martina—and Siena. So, for the first time in my life, I folded. "I promise."

It was the vow she wanted to hear, so she sighed in relief then looked out the window again.

This woman could make me do anything.

And I hated that.

———

We spent the entire day shopping. We got everything Martina could possibly need, from toys to bottles and all the other products I had no idea were required to take care of a baby. Siena had fun picking out all the clothes Martina would get to wear, and even though she was on her feet all day, she didn't complain once.

I'd never spent more than five minutes shopping. My personal stylist picked out my wardrobe then had my tailor customize it to my measurements. Then one of my men picked up the clothes and placed them in my closet.

I didn't even go grocery shopping.

After the long day, we headed home, taking the entire store with us.

"Should this be her bedroom?" Siena stepped into the guest bedroom next door to mine. My office was on the other side. "It's right next door."

"I don't think our daughter is going to want to be right next door to us."

"Not forever. Just for now. That way when she cries in the middle of the night, I don't have to go far. I think the smart thing is keeping her close." She stepped into the room and looked at the furniture that was already inside. "I guess we could donate all of this. Everything looks to be of exceptional quality. Unless you have somewhere else to put it?"

I shook my head. "No."

"Then we'll donate it to someone. I want to paint the walls and set up the crib next to the window. Do you think your men could get rid of everything tomorrow?"

"They could get rid of it now if that's what you wanted."

"God, no. It's seven at night."

"This shift is on until midnight regardless."

"So you have men working constantly?"

I nodded. "They work twelve-hour shifts."

"Do you pay them well?"

"Of course. You can't expect men to put their lives on the line unless they're giving their families the best quality of life possible. That's all they care about, making sure their wives don't have to work and their kids get the best education. Any honorable man would do anything to give his family a better life." That was all I ever wanted for my mother when my father ducked out. I wanted to erase what he did and prove what being a man really meant. "So they'll do anything I ask."

"Well, it can still wait until morning. Then we'll set up the crib and add a new coat of paint."

"I'll bring someone in to do all of that."

"Why? We can do it ourselves."

"Because rich people never do anything themselves."

She rolled her eyes. "I want to be part of the process every step of the way. I want to put my love into the paint, build that crib with my bare hands. I thought you would feel the same way…"

I hated it when she guilted me. "I have work to do, Siena. You seem to forget that a lot."

"And you seem to forget that you already have billions. You don't even need to work anymore."

"It's not just about the money."

"Whatever," she said. "I'll do it myself." She walked into our bedroom and started to undress.

I followed behind her. "Could you at least wait until I get home from work tomorrow? The guys will move the furniture during the day, and then we can take care of this when I get home."

Since I'd offered a compromise, she seemed more receptive. "Okay, that sounds fair."

———

"I got the deal—with no help from you." Bates sat in the leather armchair and lit a cigar.

"You texted me, and I texted you back."

"And you think that's work? Did you have fun picking out diapers and shit?" He tossed a cigar at me.

I caught it and set it on the desk. "I didn't mind it." I didn't care about picking out all the essentials, but knowing everything was for my daughter made it a lot more interesting. I selected a few toys for her, along with one or two outfits. It hit me more with every passing day that I was going to be a father—in a month.

He glanced at my cigar then tossed a lighter at me.

I caught it and put it on the desk next to the cigar.

Bates took in the smoke then blew rings toward the ceiling. "What's your problem?"

"Just not smoking."

"Because...?"

I shrugged. "Don't want to."

"All we ever do is smoke and drink."

"Maybe we should branch out more."

His eyes narrowed. "What's going on, Cato? We've never had these little conversations without a cigar in our hand. What gives?"

Since I would never smoke again, I might as well tell him the truth. "I quit."

He laughed like it was absurd. "Quit? You? Why?"

"Smoking kills," I said simply.

It didn't take long for my brother to figure out the real reason on his own. "Siena forced you?"

"She didn't force me. She asked me."

"My god, you're pussy-whipped so fucking hard."

I didn't deny it because it was true. "She made valid points. And she wasn't going to let it go unless I caved."

"What valid points?"

"That I should live as long as possible for Martina's sake. She's going to be born into a violent world. I'm the only one who can really protect her. Now that I'm having my kid, my priorities are changing. I wouldn't have made these sacrifices before, but now that there's something more important than me, it's easy to make these changes. Maybe one day you'll understand."

"I highly doubt that." He kept smoking. "I've been keeping an eye on Micah and Damien. Still nothing."

"If nothing has been going on this long, maybe they are shutting down the business."

"I don't buy that. They're doing something, and they don't want anyone to know about it."

"Isn't that true for all criminals?"

"But to completely disappear?" He shook his head. "That's shady."

"We're all shady," I reminded him.

"I'm not gonna drop this, man. I'm telling you, something is up."

"Maybe something is up," I said. "But maybe it has nothing to do with us."

"Everything has to do with us, Cato. We're the top of the food chain—and everything beneath us is our business." His eyes drifted away as he continued to enjoy his cigar. He pulled the smoke into his mouth then let it slowly seep out between his lips. "So, one month to go, huh?"

I nodded. "One month."

"Are you gonna kill her?"

The question surprised me. "I thought we were past this?"

He shrugged. "She still did terrible things that she wasn't punished for. Damien and Micah might suspect she means a lot to you, which would make her and your daughter primary targets."

"So killing her is the solution?" I snapped.

"Maybe," he said. "Or maybe you could just give her a scare. Punish her for everything she did. Prove to your enemies she means nothing to you."

"So, don't shoot her?"

"Just go through the motions and make her think it's happening. That terror will be punishment enough. Then she can really have a blank slate."

I actually liked that idea. People talked, so the world would know that I'd seriously considered killing her. It would make her look expendable and less valuable as a target.

"She still should be punished for what she did. Just because she has a magic pussy doesn't make her immune to justice." He sucked on his cigar again. "That's my two cents. It will give you the closure you need, and she will forgive you because she'll know you're even."

A part of me felt terrible for considering such a thing, but another part of me felt it was justified. The beginning of our relationship was a complete lie. To top it off, she ran away from me—and took my baby. They were two offenses that both deserved the death penalty. "I'll think about it."

"You've got a month—so take your time."

———

I snuck out of bed at two in the morning and headed back to Florence. Bates met me on the way, and we descended into the Underground where the Skull Kings operated—nearly in plain sight.

The security checked us at the front and made sure we were unarmed. Under my special agreement with various factions throughout the country, I was allowed to bring three armed men anywhere I went. Each one carried an assault rifle that would annihilate everyone in that room before they could draw their pistols.

We took our seats at a round table, and a topless waitress fetched us our drinks.

Bates watched her lean over and set our glasses in front of us, his eyes eating up the sight of her tits. When she walked away, his eyes followed her like he'd never seen anything more beautiful. He took a drink as he continued to watch her.

"They're just tits, Bates." I looked at the stage and saw the poor women up for auction. All naked, young, and afraid, they would be auctioned off to the highest bidder for an unspeakable existence. I knew how the Skull Kings made their money, and even though I was opposed to it, I didn't intervene. Unless a woman explicitly wanted sex, I wasn't interested. I didn't get off on the idea of forcing a woman to please me. Sex with an eager partner was so much better. But all the sick fucks in this room didn't agree with me, and even if I had the power to save the lives of these women, I wouldn't bother.

"But nice fucking tits. Probably fake but who gives a damn."

I looked into my glass and took a drink, ignoring the auction that carried on around us. An older man bid on a woman who couldn't be a day over twenty. Another man raised his paddle and increased the stakes. Back and forth they went until the older man won his prize.

Claw lowered himself into the seat across from us, the scar still visible down his left cheek. He was the top dog of the organization, the cruelest one of the bunch. "Glad you could make it, gentlemen. We have a lot of beauties for sale."

"Is she for sale?" Bates nodded to the waitress.

"Ask her that, and she'll cut off your balls." Claw laughed maniacally before he drank from his glass—straight vodka. "So, how can I help the Marino Brothers? I heard you're expecting a little one, Cato. Congratulations."

I didn't appear disgruntled by his knowledge. "Thank you. I'm having a girl."

"Not a boy to take over the empire?"

"There's still time to make one."

Claw winked and clinked his glass against mine. "Then what brings you here? Looking for another woman to give you a son?"

"Just here to check on our investment." I crossed my legs, and my elbow rested on the table. "You've borrowed a lot of money from me, and I hope you're on track for paying it back."

"You don't need to play the banker with me," Claw said. "We always pay. You know that."

"And I always check," I countered. "You know that."

His smile faded. "Don't worry another minute about it, Cato. Production is going smoothly. Once we sell our first batch, that'll be more than enough to pay you back in full —along with your interest rate."

"Good." I clinked my glass against his. "Glad to hear. Loaning nearly a billion dollars overall to one group is pretty generous. We don't do that for just anyone."

"We don't," Bates said in agreement. "And on that note, what do you know about Micah and Damien?"

Normally, I would roll my eyes or tell Bates to shut his mouth, but in the presence of Claw, I had to roll with the punches. It was a stupid question to ask, a question that was wasted.

"Haven't spoken to Damien in a while." Claw leaned back in his chair. "It doesn't seem like they're distributing drugs the way they used to. Maybe there's a bigger player that's come to town."

"Then where are you getting your fix?" Bates blurted.

I intimidated my allies and my enemies. But I didn't interrogate them.

"I get my fix everywhere," Claw said. "But you know what my biggest fix is right now?" He grinned widely. "Pussy. Lots of pussy. The ones that aren't virgins go through a strict quality-control check by us before they get on that stage." He nodded behind him.

Before Bates could fixate on his obsession with Damien and Micah any longer, I kicked him under the table.

Bates clenched his jaw but didn't make a sound.

"Your next payment is due in a month. Hope you deliver on time." I finished my drink before I rose to my feet. "Until next time."

"You aren't gonna buy a bitch for the road?" he asked, not rising to his feet.

Bates stood up and pulled out a business card with his phone number written on it. "Let the bartender know I'm looking for a good lay if she is."

"And I'll pass," I said. "I don't pay millions for pussy."

I didn't pay for pussy at all anymore. There was only one woman in my bed—and only one woman I wanted in my bed.

———

Siena called me on the way home. "Where the hell are you?"

I was just down the street from my estate. I'd hoped I would be able to slip in and out without her noticing I was gone. I liked having a woman to come home to at night, but I hated having someone to answer to whenever I left. There was no way around it, none that I could see. "I'm down the street. I'll be home in five minutes."

"Is everything alright?" she asked, desperation in her voice.

"Yes, baby." I spoke in a bored tone, but I liked hearing the concern in her voice. It was the same sensation I felt when she said she loved me. She had me wrapped around her finger, and I loved knowing she was wrapped around mine.

"Then why are you sneaking out in the middle of the night?"

"I'm not sneaking. Just didn't want to wake you."

"But why are you leaving the house in the middle of the night?"

"Work."

"Work?" she asked. "It's almost four."

"Which is early if you ask me."

She growled into the phone then hung up.

Wow, she hung up on me. She really was pissed.

I loved it when she was pissed.

I arrived at the house minutes later then entered the bedroom. She sat up against the headboard, her large stomach stretching my t-shirt. Without looking at her, I stripped off each piece of my suit.

She walked up to me, the fire still burning in her eyes. She opened her mouth to say something but then shut it again once she smelled something in the air. "Why do you smell like smoke, booze, and perfume?"

"Because I was at an underground auction."

"A what?" she asked.

"It's a place where rich men buy women."

She crossed her arms over her chest, her attitude in full force. "And why you were there?"

"I told you. Work."

"Uh-huh."

"You think I snuck out in the middle of the night to cheat on you?" I asked incredulously. "If I wanted to fuck another woman, I would do it. You could watch for all I care. I can do whatever I want."

Her eyes dropped their hostility. "Did you smoke?"

"I promised you I wouldn't. But I can't stop other people from doing it—including Bates."

Her anger started to dim further. "Then what were you working on?"

"The Skull Kings took out another loan from me. I was just checking up on it."

"Did they miss a payment?"

"No. But that's not how it works. I drop in on all my clients —to remind them what will happen if they don't pay me back when they're supposed to."

"What?" she asked. "You kill these people?"

I didn't blink. "Yes."

"If you're that concerned about it, don't loan your money in the first place."

"I make too much off it. This deal alone puts two hundred million in my pocket."

She rolled her eyes. "What's two hundred million to a man worth six billion? Do you understand how ridiculous you sound?"

"You're the one who's ridiculous. Everyone in the world wants money. You're the only one who doesn't." I finished removing my suit and tossed it into the hamper. I dropped my boxers next, semi-hard because her anger turned me on.

"So you make these deals for money, catch them off guard in the middle of the night, and threaten them? That sounds like too much work, too much risk for someone who's so rich. It's beneath you, Cato. You should just walk away while you still can."

"Not gonna happen."

"You will put Martina in danger every time until you do. Just something to think about." She glanced at my dick. "And you better put on some boxers because I'm not fucking you tonight. Not after that stunt." She went back to bed and got under the sheets.

"That's what you think." I turned off the light and got into bed beside her.

"I'm serious."

"You're mad at me for doing my job?"

"I'm mad at you for sneaking off in the middle of the night while I'm pregnant and alone."

"You have fifty men here."

"They aren't *you*, Cato." She pushed me off her and turned onto her side. "Now, go to sleep."

"You really think I would ever put you two in danger?" I grabbed her shoulder and rolled her to her back again. "No. Never." I moved to my knees and placed myself between her thighs. "And I want to fuck you like this as much as I can. This next month is going to go by fast—and there won't be sex for six weeks."

6

SIENA

Martina's room was exactly what I wanted it to be.

The walls were painted pastel purple, the crib was pearl white, and her changing station and toys were all set up. The room was filled with so much love for a baby who hadn't even been born yet. A rocking chair sat in the corner, and I imagined that's where I would rock her to sleep in the middle of the night. Her mouth would latch on to my breast, and I would feel her in the most primal way.

I took a seat in the chair and rocked myself, holding the stuffed giraffe Cato had picked out for her. He hadn't been that interested in shopping when we were at the store, but he found a few items that resonated with him. One of them was the giraffe—and a set of pajamas he liked.

I didn't know why I got so upset with Cato last week. When I realized I was the only one in bed, I got scared. I worried something had happened to him, that something might happen to me. I called him in near hysterics, and then when he came home smelling like booze and women, I let my insecurities get to me.

My body had changed so much with the pregnancy. My stomach was enormous, my thighs were thick, and I was in so much discomfort, I wasn't the carefree and spontaneous woman I used to be.

Cato was used to an endless line of beautiful women.

I feared he'd gotten tired of me.

I believed he loved me, but the hormones made me crazy sometimes.

Cato opened the door in his sweatpants, his eyes scanning for me like he'd been looking for me throughout the house. He spotted me slowly rocking in the chair with the giraffe held to my chest. "Should have known you'd be in here." He stepped inside and walked past the crib as he came close to me. Perfectly chiseled without an ounce of fat on his body, he was as gorgeous as ever. Even if he weren't a billionaire, he could have whatever woman he wanted. Supermodels…yoga instructors…anyone.

"I like it in here. Peaceful."

He rested one hand on the crib as he watched me rock back and forth. "Can I join you?"

"You're very fit, but I don't think I can hold you."

He smiled. "You know what I mean."

"I don't know...I think I'm too big."

He rolled his eyes like I was being ridiculous. "Get up."

I moved to my feet then he sat down.

Slowly, I lowered myself onto his lap, my legs resting across his. I held the giraffe against my belly.

Cato supported me with his arms and gently rocked us both with his foot. "You're right. It is peaceful in here."

"It won't be after she's born," I said with a chuckle. "There will be lots of crying and screaming."

"Not much different than it is now," he teased.

I smiled and smacked him playfully on the arm. "I scream a lot. But I don't cry."

He moved his lips to my hairline and gave me a soft kiss.

It was a sweet, affectionate gesture, the kind that made me close my eyes and feel the warmth in my chest. It made me feel special, knowing he'd never done that to another woman. "I feel so uncomfortable right now..."

His hand moved to my stomach. "I know, baby. But it'll be over soon."

"I feel so fat...so ugly."

He gave a sarcastic snort. "What the hell are you talking about? You're pregnant, not fat."

"Whatever. I'm huge. When you went out last week...I guess I was scared that you were..." I didn't finish the sentence, feeling too guilty to say the words out loud. I never thought I would be the insecure type, to constantly accuse their partner of cheating just because I had no self-esteem.

"What?" he pressed.

"Don't make me say it."

"No, I'm gonna." He grabbed my chin and forced me to look at him. "What did you think I snuck off in the middle of the night to do?"

The guilt smothered my words so I looked away. "I know the kind of lifestyle you're used to. I know the kind of women you like."

"For the last ten months, I've been with the same woman every single night. I've watched my daughter grow inside her belly, and with every passing day, I've become hotter for her. The way your back arches, the way that stomach protrudes, the glow in your eyes...sexiest thing in the world. Trust me, my eyes don't wander. Whenever I have a moment to myself at work, I'm thinking about you. I'm thinking about getting home as quickly as I can so I can be with you." His fingers moved under my chin and forced me to look at him again. "I'm an honest man. If I want another woman, I would tell you. But I really don't—just you."

Tears hit my eyes, and I blinked them away quickly so they would stop. My attempts to ward them off weren't good enough, and they pierced through my eyes and dripped down my cheeks. "I'm sorry I got jealous."

"It's okay," he whispered. "It turns me on when you get jealous."

I wiped my tears away with my fingertips. "I thought insecurity would be ugly."

"Not with you. You could walk into any bar, right now, and pick up a handsome guy. The fact that you're spending your time worrying about me instead of finding someone better is sexy. You're needy, possessive, jealous...and I like it."

———

Bates was walking into the house when I reached the last stair. "Damn, you're huge."

I gripped the rail as I made my way downstairs, taking my time because the extra weight was painful on my joints. "Thanks."

"I didn't know women could get that big." He stared at my stomach like it defied logic. "Can you even bend over?"

"Yes. And I can also kick you in the nuts."

He covered his crotch with his hands and stepped back. "Whoa, let's calm down. I wasn't trying to be insulting."

"Well, you were extremely insulting." If Cato hadn't reinvigorated my self-esteem, I would probably be in tears right now. "Why are you here?"

"Work. Cato and I have a conference call."

"Oh..." If I had it my way, Cato would retire. But talking him into that was impossible. Even if he did it, he would probably resent me for it. "Where do you live, anyway?" I had no idea where Bates's residence was. Did he live in Florence? Did he live in Tuscany?

"Why? You wanna come over?" He waggled his eyebrows.

"You nearly broke my nose just outside this house. So, no."

"Hey, that was nothing personal. That's just how we treat traitors."

"And you're lucky I won't tell Cato you made a pass at me."

"I didn't make a pass," he argued. "Unless you're saying yes..." He waggled his eyebrows again.

"I really am going to kick you in the crotch."

He stepped back farther. "I live a few miles away from my mother. So, I live in Tuscany. I've got a big, beautiful house just like Cato. My chef isn't quite as good, but she's nice to me, so whatever."

"That must be pretty hard to do...be nice to you."

"I've been told that before." He slid his hands into the pockets of his suit.

"Why are you being so nice to me?" I blurted, surprised we were having a somewhat civil conversation.

"You think this is nice? You should see me with my ladies."

"It's definitely an improvement over being called a manipulative gold digger all the time."

"Not to mention whore, bitch, and dumb bitch." He counted all the names on his fingers. "But signing those papers really proved yourself to me. You excused yourself from any kind of inheritance from Cato. So, if you really are only with him for the money, there's no point in sticking around at this point. "I'm not saying I like you since you did betray my brother, but I don't want to snap your neck anymore either."

"Oh good," I said sarcastically. "I feel so much better now…"

"You should. This is me making an effort to be somewhat nice to you. But not too nice…can't have that."

"Even though I'm giving birth to your niece?"

"Regardless of who gives birth, she's still my niece. Blood is blood."

"Your niece will have half my blood, so that means you and I will be family."

He shook his head. "The only way we'll be family is if Cato marries you. And that'll never happen." He walked past me and headed to the office where he and Cato usually met.

Getting married had never been important to me, but now that Martina was almost here, I wished Cato and I were something more. I wished he would tell me he loved me. I wished he weren't just the father of my child…but also my husband. But I couldn't rush Cato into anything. If I questioned him about it, I would only be met with his silence.

Cato walked out of the kitchen, dressed casually in jeans and a t-shirt. "Everything alright?"

"Your brother is waiting for you in the office."

Cato knew me better than anyone, even my own brother. He could read my body language like it was words written on a page. Even feelings I tried to hide from him somehow got pulled to the surface. "What did he say to you?"

"Nothing."

He didn't believe me at all. "What did he say, Siena?"

"Nothing that I want to disclose." I moved past him. "I'll see you later."

———

I couldn't sleep at all.

She was kicking so hard. In the beginning, it was cute, but now it was just annoying. Her feet slammed on my belly constantly, my feet were so swollen, and everything hurt. It didn't matter what the AC was set to, I was always hot. I became so uncomfortable that I didn't even want sex, which was shocking since my lover was Cato, the most beautiful man in the world.

I rolled from side to side then eventually settled on my back. I breathed through the discomfort and fantasized about it being over. Labor would be painful and terrifying, and even when I returned from the hospital, I would be sore and exhausted. On top of that, I would have to take care of a crying baby nonstop. I had a long way to go before I had a good night's sleep.

I suddenly felt a sensation between my legs, a flood of wetness that dripped over my thighs and to the mattress beneath me. "Oh god…" Both of my hands flew to my stomach as the panic settled in.

Cato was instantly awake at my words. "Baby, what is it? What's wrong?" He opened his eyes, and his hand flew to my stomach.

"My water just broke…"

He stilled at the announcement, taking it in while half asleep. Then he sprang into action. "Alright. Let's get you to the hospital." He grabbed his phone off the nightstand and told his men to prepare the car for the hospital. Then he called someone and told them to prepare for my arrival. He pulled on jeans and a t-shirt with a jacket then helped me change into my clothes for the hospital.

"I can't believe this is happening…"

"She's here, baby." He helped me slip on my shoes. "She's coming. All we have to do is push her out."

I scoffed. "You mean, *I* have to push her out. As if that's going to be easy."

"Easy or hard, you will do it." He stood upright then got my jacket around my shoulders. "The hardest part is coming, but soon, it'll all be over. The three of us will be home in no time." He grabbed my bag from the dresser and then took me by the hand. "It'll be alright, I promise."

————

By the time I arrived at the hospital, the contractions had started.

And Jesus, they were painful.

I was put into a room right away with the nurses and the doctor, and after my examination, they said she was already coming.

"Wait, aren't I supposed to sit around for like ten hours before I go into real labor?" I wasn't prepared to give birth right this second. Everything was moving so fast. I was about to be a mother. *Oh my god, I'm about to be a mother.*

"No, the baby is coming now," the doctor said. "I'm going to need you to start pushing."

I looked at Cato, like I expected him to fix this somehow.

He stood at my bedside and held my hand. "She doesn't like to waste time. She's definitely my daughter."

"I don't think I can do it." I looked into his blue eyes and admitted my weakness. I was usually strong, regardless of the situation, but right now, I was terrified. "My mom's not here, and I always thought she would be here... I can't do this. I can't push this person out of my body. It's not physically possible."

"Baby, baby." He gripped my hand. "Calm down."

"You calm down," I hissed.

"I'm sorry your mother couldn't be here, but I am here. We'll get through this together. There's no time to be scared, Siena. Our daughter needs you to push, so you need to start pushing. Think about her."

That seemed to be the exact advice I needed. Now that she was coming into the world, I wasn't important anymore. She was the most important thing in our lives, and instead of giving in to the fear, I needed to get her into my arms as quickly as possible. "Alright...I can do it."

"I know you can, baby."

———

Hours later, she arrived.

The doctor cleaned her up and wrapped her in a warm pink blanket before he carried her to me. She was crying at the top of her lungs, but the sound didn't irritate me at all. It was a normal reaction when entering the cold air of the world. "Here she is." He handed her over.

My body was exhausted from the labor. My legs shook from pushing so hard, and I was tired from not sleeping well for the last few nights. But the hard part was over—and my reward was finally given to me.

I would never forget this moment, holding my daughter for the very first time. "Martina..." I held her with both arms and looked at her tiny fingers. She still cried hysterically, but my ears seemed to automatically morph into mom ears, able to handle the high-pitched cries. Her eyes were closed because she hadn't opened them just yet, and I waited to see their color. I hoped she had Cato's eyes. I wanted to see him every time I looked at her.

Her eyes opened—and they were blue like the ocean.

"Just like your father." I brought her head to my mouth and kissed her forehead. "You're so perfect." I stared into her face with a permanent smile on my lips. Slowly, her cries stopped as she became just as entertained by looking at me as I was looking at her.

I'd had a special relationship with my mother, and it broke my heart that she wasn't here for this moment. I'd always assumed she would teach me everything about being a mom—because she was the best mom in the world. I knew she would be overjoyed to see her granddaughter, to babysit her as much as possible so I could have time off with Cato. But she wasn't here...and I was starting my own family without her.

Cato stood over me and stared at Martina in silence. He was silent and still, taking in the moment with an expression that was impossible to read. He didn't seem happy or sad. He seemed...overwhelmed. One moment, it was just the two of us, and then it became the three of us. This little girl had been the result of an accident, but that accident turned into the best thing to ever happen to us. She saved my life...and she made Cato into a better man.

"You want to hold her?" I whispered.

Like he hadn't heard a word I said, he continued to stand there. He didn't extend his arms or give any indication he'd heard me. His breathing was deep and heavy, the emotion clearly flooding his veins. He finally came to terms with his thoughts and extended his arms to make the transfer.

I placed her in his arms and let go.

Cato held her with a single arm because she was so small in comparison to his size. He moved his other hand under her head then lifted her toward his face so he could get a closer look at her.

Martina didn't cry. Only faint coos came from her little mouth.

I watched them together, watched the weight of the moment overcome Cato. The instant I went into labor, the reality of my life hit me hard. But it didn't happen for him until he saw her face for the first time.

"Sweetheart, you're beautiful," he whispered to her, having a private conversation between father and daughter. "Just like your mother." He brought her forehead to his lips and kissed her the way I had.

I felt the tears burn in my eyes. It didn't matter how much pain I was in or how exhausted I was. This scene moved me to tears.

He held her close to his face and spoke again. "I promise I'll never leave you, sweetheart. No matter what. I'll always take care of you. I'll always protect you. And every night, I will always come home."

———

When we went home the next day, I was exhausted. I was constantly feeding her and rocking her back to sleep so she would stop crying. If I weren't so tired, I would just keep going, but I'd reached my limit.

Cato put her in the crib next door and joined me in the bedroom, but her wails were so loud, they couldn't be ignored. With the doors open, a baby monitor was unnecessary.

"I can't let her cry like that." I pushed the sheets back.

"Baby, rest." Cato put me back in bed and pulled the sheets to my shoulder.

"She needs me, and I know you have work tomorrow."

"I took a few days off. I'll take care of her so you can get your strength back."

Cato Marino, the billionaire banker, took time off to take care of his daughter? "I thought you were going to get a nanny or something?"

"Eventually. But for now, I think it's best if we're the ones taking care of her. It's important for bonding. I don't want Martina to come into this world and be cared for by a stranger. It should be us."

A wide smile melted across my face. "I know I'm super tired right now...but you are Cato, right?"

He smiled and pulled the sheets to my shoulder. "I've got her. You just rest. You grew a person inside your body for nine months and then pushed her out. You've done enough."

I gripped his hand. "If I weren't a nightmare down below, I'd be fucking your brains out right now."

He chuckled then kissed my palm. "You can make it up to me later."

7

CATO

I was a father.

As Siena grew bigger over the last few months, the inevitable truth looked me right in the face. Then I watched her do the most difficult thing any woman could —give birth. After lots of screaming and lots of pain, my daughter arrived.

And my life would never be the same.

She was beautiful, healthy, and perfect.

I would never forget the moment I held her in my arms for the first time. All I wanted to do was protect her, hide her away from all the terrible things in life. I only wanted her to see kittens and rainbows. That moment changed me, for better or worse. I was filled with love but also hatred. How could my father ever hold me and then walk out? How could he turn his back on his two sons without feeling dead inside?

I could never do that to Martina.

Regardless of the sleepless nights, the dirty diapers, the stains she would leave all over my clothes, she was still my family—and you never turned your back on family. I took her into her bedroom and rocked her in the chair, unsure what else to do with her. She wasn't old enough to talk, just old enough to stare at me.

I stared back.

When she was quiet like this, being a parent felt like the easiest thing in the world. But I knew this peace wouldn't last forever. The road ahead would be difficult, and I would have to learn so many things. I didn't even know how to change a diaper.

Thank god for YouTube.

———

When Siena woke up, she stayed in bed and had dinner on a tray. I sat in a chair by her bedside with Martina in my arms. She was so small she could easily fit into just a single arm. With her little fingers and little toes, it was difficult to believe she would grow up to be a woman someday.

"How was she?" Siena's hair was pulled back, and even though she'd slept all day, she still looked exhausted. Her body must still be in disarray after pushing out another person. Her eyes were filled with such fatigue that it seemed like she hadn't slept at all.

"There were a few hours when she wouldn't stop crying. I fed her, changed her, rocked her...nothing worked."

"Maybe she was cold?"

"I don't know. But she stopped eventually. The rest of the time, I just held her in the rocking chair. She stared at me and I stared at her."

Siena smiled. "That sounds nice."

Martina started to cry a second later, her wails so loud, they nearly shook the walls.

"Not so nice anymore," I said with a chuckle.

"She's probably hungry." She moved the tray aside then lifted up her shirt to reveal her swollen tit. "I'm uncomfortable anyway." She took Martina from my hands and positioned her at her breast.

Martina latched on right away.

I watched Siena breastfeed our child, and now everything felt even more real.

Siena watched our daughter for a long time, affection in her eyes and a smile on her lips. "I can keep her. I'm sure there's stuff you need to do."

"I'd like to hit the gym and take a shower."

"Okay. Sounds good."

I stayed in my seat and continued to watch them together, mother and daughter. It was hard to believe I'd created something so beautiful and innocent, but I was sure Martina had inherited those qualities from her mother. She had my eyes, and hopefully, she would have my strength and fierceness. I wouldn't raise her to believe in fairy tales or Prince Charming. I would raise her to be her own warrior, to never settle for anything less than what she deserved. One day, a man would come to me asking for her hand, and I wouldn't give her away unless that man was twice the man I was.

Siena studied me. "What are you thinking about?"

The question broke my concentration. "Father stuff...stuff I shouldn't have to worry about for a long time."

————

By the fourth day, I understood Martina's needs a lot better. Her cries always sounded the same to me, but the time of day gave clues to what she needed. Changing diapers was easy, feeding her from the bottle was even easier. Once she got comfortable in the house, she started to sleep a lot more.

Those were my favorite moments.

I went into my office and sat in the leather armchair behind my desk. My laptop was open in front of me, but the liquor cabinet was closed tight. I would normally be drinking or smoking in here, but now that I had a daughter, the things I loved were put on the back burner—because I loved her more.

I leaned back in the chair so my chest was flat, and Martina slept on her stomach right against me. The position wasn't that comfortable for me, but that was how she liked to take her midday naps. I typed on my computer and responded to a few emails.

Bates called me.

I answered with a soft voice. "Yes?"

"What do you mean *yes*? I see that you're working. Ready to come back to the office?"

Siena had nearly recovered from labor, but I was giving her as much time as she needed to get back on her feet. Taking care of Martina for most of the day allowed her to relax. So far, she hadn't changed a diaper once. "Not for a few more days."

"Why?"

"Because I'm taking care of Martina right now. Siena is still resting."

"Cato, that's what nannies are for. And they're dirt cheap."

Thankfully, Martina stayed asleep for the entire conversation. Perhaps she liked listening to the sound of my voice. "I don't want a nanny, Bates. I want to be the one to take care of her."

"You want to change diapers?" he said incredulously. "Wipe butts?"

"Yes. And yes."

He scoffed into the phone. "I don't get you, man. You're this powerful banker, but you're at home with a brat drooling all over you."

"Don't call her that," I warned. "You'll need facial reconstruction if you do."

"Then when are you coming back?"

"You know, paternity leave is at least three months."

"No, asshole. You aren't skipping out for three months."

"I know," I said. "But I'm just reminding you what the rest of the country does. Besides, you can handle it on your own, Bates. You really don't need me. When your time comes, I won't need you."

"When my time comes?" he blurted. "No, I always wear a condom."

"When you fall in love, you'll stop wearing a condom."

He turned dead silent.

It took me several seconds to understand the source of his silence, how my poorly chosen words were misinterpreted. "I'm just saying..."

Bates didn't revisit the comment, but it was awkward for the rest of the conversation. "Why are you doing all the work?"

"Because she was pregnant for nine months and pushed a human out of her. She deserves a week off."

"She's the mother," he argued. "She should be taking care of her kid."

"Stop being a sexist bitch."

"Sexist?" he asked. "See, this is why I don't like Siena. She puts these stupid thoughts in your head."

"It's not because of her. I have a daughter now—and I see the world differently because of it. By the way, you haven't asked to see her once."

"You know I'm not a baby person."

"But this is your niece. Your family. She might be the closest thing to a daughter you ever have."

"God, I hope so," he said with a sigh. "I'll talk to Mother, and we'll stop by. I know she's eager to see you guys. She calls me every day, trying to figure out when it's appropriate to nag you."

"She's never cared about an appropriate time to nag me before."

"I think she's thinking of Siena."

Of course. My mother didn't have any boundaries with me. "Siena has been feeling a lot better, so I'm sure she'll be ready for visitors tomorrow."

"Alright. By the way, are you going to do that thing we talked about?"

Drag Siena outside and put her on her knees to be executed. To scare her so senseless it'd be the best punishment for the two crimes she'd committed. She'd never paid for what she did, other than the time my brother bloodied her. Just a few days after that, I fetched her father's body from my enemies and called a truce just to have him. Siena never suffered for what she did. Right off the bat, she softened my anger, and I took care of her. "I haven't decided yet."

"Well, I hope you do it. I'm much more civil to her, but I would be willing to give her a clean slate if she were fairly punished for what she did. We all have to pay the price for our sins—Siena Russo is no different."

———

I lay in bed beside Siena, the baby in between us.

Siena had her head propped up on her hand as she rubbed Martina's stomach. Her eyes were downcast as she looked at our daughter, sleeping between us so nothing could ever happen to her. Siena smiled as she stared at Martina, watching her little chest rise and fall as she slept. "Can you believe how perfect she is?" she whispered in the dark.

"No."

"Healthy, beautiful, happy...she's the perfect baby."

"Wait and see how you feel when you're changing her diaper all day, listening to her cry nonstop for an hour, and letting her sleep on your chest so you can't move for a few hours."

Her eyes lifted to me with the same smile. "Still perfect. And you think she's perfect too."

I didn't deny it. "I do. My mother and brother want to come over tomorrow for a visit. Are you up for it?"

"Yeah. I'm surprised they didn't come sooner."

"Wanted to give you time to recover."

"I'll invite Landon too. He's been blowing up my phone lately. Wants to meet his niece."

I wished my brother shared the same enthusiasm. "They'll be here at noon."

"Sounds good." She lowered her head back to the pillow with her face close to Martina. She closed her eyes and kept her fingers on Martina's stomach, feeling her breathe like she needed that assurance to sleep. "Thanks for taking care of her. It's been so nice to rest. When we came home, I felt like I'd been hit by a train."

"I can only imagine."

"I know taking care of a baby by yourself couldn't have been easy, so thank you."

"I didn't do it alone. I asked Giovanni lots of questions."

She chuckled. "Thank goodness we have him. He can do more than cook."

"That guy can do everything. That's why I hired him."

She kept her eyes closed, and her fingers stopped rubbing Martina's tummy. "I wish we didn't have to wait six weeks…"

I'd been so busy taking care of Martina, I hadn't thought about sex much. That little baby became the center of my universe, and all the things that used to matter stopped being important. I didn't care about sex, booze, or work. All I cared about was changing diapers and putting a bottle in her mouth. "It'll be over before you know it."

"Yeah...I guess. I just know—"

"Don't worry about me, baby. I'm not going anywhere."

———

"Oh my god, she's the most precious thing." Mother held her on the couch in the living room, her arms enveloping Martina in a warm gray blanket. "Aww...she has your eyes, honey." She held her against her shoulder and gently swayed her from side to side. "She's so perfect."

Bates sat beside her, looking at the baby like he wasn't entirely sure what it was.

Mother hogged Martina for a long time, ignoring the other two people who were there to see her. She patted the back of Martina's head and hummed quietly under her breath like she was singing her to sleep.

I sat beside Siena on the other couch, my hand on her thigh. "Mother."

"Oh, sorry," she said as she handed the baby to Bates. "I'm just so happy to be a grandmother. You got her, honey?"

Bates moved his arms underneath her body then held her the way my mother did. "Like this?" He held her still and looked down into her face. "Hey, she does have my eyes." He looked up and winked at Siena.

"You wanna die?" I threatened.

"Chill." Bates looked down into Martina's face. "I'm your uncle. When your father is driving you crazy, come to me. I'll tell you how to handle him. Thank god you look like your mom. Cato as a woman would not be attractive." He carried Martina to Landon next.

Landon was a lot more affectionate. "Hey, beautiful." He leaned back in the armchair and held her close to his body, looking down into her face. "I see so much of my sister in you...and my mother." Landon smiled as he looked at her, something he didn't seem capable of doing. He was rigid and cold the way I was, but Martina broke down his walls —just the way she did with me.

Siena moved to the spot beside him, and they looked at her together. "I wish Mama were here."

"Me too," he said sadly. "Father too."

"Yeah..."

"But we're starting our own families," Landon said. "You'll have more babies, and maybe I'll have some kids. Then our family can grow."

"I thought you were a terminal bachelor?" she teased.

"Who said I won't be?" he countered. "Doesn't mean I can't have some kids. You and Cato aren't married, and you have a family."

Siena lifted her gaze and looked at me. Affection was in her eyes, along with a drop of sadness. Then she looked down at our daughter once more, brushing off the moment. "True. You can still be a family."

8

SIENA

I worried what life would be like once Martina arrived. I didn't know how Cato would respond to her, if he wouldn't connect with the baby and then push us both away. I never expected him to take care of her for an entire week just so I could recover.

That man had a big heart.

A week of recovery helped me get back on my feet. My body didn't ache as much anymore, and labor finally seemed like a distant memory. I had the energy to take care of Martina in the middle of the night, to feed her and rock her so Cato could get some rest.

After everything he'd done for me, I didn't mind in the least.

It felt so good to take care of her, to feel like a mother. For the week I rested, I felt like a terrible mother. Even though I knew I needed to recover, I still felt guilty that I wasn't the one spending time with her. Now that I was, my life felt complete.

She was the sweetest thing in the world.

I already wanted another one.

Landon and I were close in age, and I wanted the same for my children. I wanted them to experience the same challenges in life at the same time so those moments could bring them closer together. If something ever happened to Cato or me, I wanted them to always have each other—the way I always had Landon.

After giving her dinner and rocking her to sleep, I placed her in the crib.

She opened her eyes to look at me, to make sure I was still there, before she closed them again.

I loved sleeping with her, but I wanted to begin the separation process sooner rather than later. I wanted her to be independent, to get used to being alone without being scared. And in six weeks, the last thing I wanted was someone in between Cato and me...because we wanted our alone time.

Cato stepped into the room and lingered in the doorway.

I looked up and saw him in the darkness, but I didn't speak out of fear of waking Martina.

His shadowed frame was difficult to make out, but those powerful shoulders were impossible to deny. He was rigid and stern, his silence somehow full of inexplicable hostility.

It must have been my imagination, because there wasn't a single reason Cato could be upset with me. The last two weeks had been wonderful. He'd returned to work because I was strong enough to take care of Martina on my own. By the time he came home, Martina was so happy to see him. The second he walked in the door, he picked her up and looked at her like she'd been on his mind all day—not me.

Once Martina was asleep, I walked toward the doorway and got a better view of his expression. It was cold, guarded, and dangerous. As if we were eight months in the past, the cruel and bitter man had returned. His jaw was clenched in a way it hadn't been in a long time. His blue eyes weren't so pretty anymore.

He stepped out of the bedroom and into the hallway.

I shut the door behind me. "What's wrong—"

He grabbed me by the elbow and yanked me down the hallway.

"Cato, what the hell are you doing?" I tried to twist out of his grasp, but it was too strong. He gripped me with the force of steel. "Cato!" I used all my body weight to get out of his hold, to get free of this man I didn't know.

"I'm doing what I promised I would do." He pulled me down the stairs.

Panic exploded inside me as the adrenaline circulated in my veins. Fear rang like a drum with every beat of my heart. I'd forgotten about his promise because it seemed irrelevant. He and I were different now. We loved each other. We had a daughter together. "You can't be serious." I pushed him off me and lost my footing.

He caught me before I fell, only to keep dragging me. "I am serious."

Tears flooded my eyes, not from terror, but anger. "I'm the mother of your child—"

"Doesn't matter."

"You can't take me away from her!" Now I fought with everything I had, fought to get back to my little girl. "How dare you? What the hell is wrong with you?"

He continued to pull me down the stairs until we reached the entryway. "You betrayed me—twice. Let's not forget that."

"Only a pathetic man holds on to the past like that." Tears ran down my cheeks like two warm rivers. "I love you and you love me. How could you do this to me? I make you happy—"

"Not happy enough." He pulled me through the front door and into the chilly nighttime air. His men were gathered around, armed with guns. Bates was there too, smiling like this was the happiest day of his life.

I kicked Cato. "You're better than this!"

He didn't react to the hit. "No one crosses Cato Marino."

"And no one gets close to him either. I feel sorry for you. I'm the one about to die—but you're the person I pity."

He left me on the concrete in front of the fountain. "Kneel."

I spat in his face. "Fuck. You."

He let the spit drip down his face until it left his chin. "I will make you, Siena. You don't want that."

I drew my hand back and slapped him across the face. "She will never forgive you. She will hate you. And I hate you." I slapped him again, putting all my weight and ferocity into the hit. I'd never wanted to hurt him so much. If I had a gun, I wouldn't hesitate to shoot him. "I can't believe I ever loved you. I'm ashamed that I did."

He grabbed my shoulders and pushed me down. "Kneel."

I let my knees buckle underneath me, and I fell to the concrete. The bullet wound in my head would drain my blood into the fountain and join all his other victims. My body would be thrown into a pit somewhere in the countryside. My daughter wouldn't remember me, not even the sound of my voice. The tears fell harder, and the cramps started in my sides.

Cato walked back to his brother and took the pistol offered to him.

I lifted my gaze and stared down the barrel, refusing to be weak in my final moments of life. I'd run away from this man because I'd feared this would be my fate. But then I fell for those blue eyes and those hot kisses. I slept beside him every night and fell deeper in love. For him to do this to me, despite all that, told me he was a psychopath. Putting up the Christmas tree meant nothing to him. The ornament I gave him meant nothing to him. The bracelet I wore on my wrist that very moment didn't mean a damn thing. "You'll regret this, Cato. My memory will haunt you every day for the rest of your life. You won't be able to look at her without thinking of me. When she grows into a beautiful woman, you'll see my face every fucking day—and you'll hate yourself for what you did."

He continued to point the gun at me. "Tell me you're sorry."

"Sorry?" I hissed. "I'm about to be shot, and you want me to apologize to you? Asshole, I'm not sorry. I'm not sorry that I lied to you to save my father. I'm not sorry I ran away to save my life. You call me a traitor, but I'm a survivor. And I would do it all over again in a heartbeat. So fucking shoot me. Just fucking do it."

He held the gun steady with his finger on the trigger. His expression was relaxed but angry. There didn't seem to be any conflict in his gaze, no pain over the decision he had to make. There was no remorse for what he was about to do.

How did I fall in love with someone so evil?

Then Cato lowered the gun. "You've served your punishment. You can get up now."

I stayed on my knees because the fear hadn't passed just yet. A second ago, a gun had been pointed at me, and I thought my life would end. I would never see my daughter grow up, never attend her wedding. And then it turned out to be some sick punishment for the things I'd done. "You fucking—"

Bates drew his pistol, aimed at my head, and pulled the trigger.

Everything went black.

9

CATO

The gunshot rang in the air.

Siena collapsed to the ground. Blood seeped from her wound.

She didn't move.

I'd seen everything that happened, but I couldn't process the violence that had just occurred right in front of me. I'd executed hundreds of people in this very spot, and not once had I'd been so deeply disturbed. But now all the air left my lungs, and I couldn't move a single inch.

Bates shot her.

So much rage. It was explosive, violent. I'd had my brother's back until the end of time, but that loyalty had been severed in a single second. He tricked me into doing this, tricked me into this ruse so he could kill her himself.

My instinct was to draw my weapon and kill him right then and there.

But Siena all that mattered.

I sprinted to her in front of the fountain. "Siena!" I cupped her face and checked her pulse.

She was still alive.

Blood matted her hair and hid the wound from view. I pulled it back and tried to examine the damage. "Baby, come on!" There was too much blood for me to see what happened, how deep the bullet went. "Get the car! Now! Someone tell Giovanni to watch the baby!"

My men worked to pull the car around so I could get to the hospital, and one ran inside to alert Giovanni.

"She'll be fine," Bates said. "I just grazed her scalp."

I lifted Siena from the ground and carried her to the car. My arms were shaking from the fury deep inside my veins. It didn't matter how mild the wound was. He'd fucking shot her. I slid her into the back seat then gave him a look full of threat. "When I get back, I will kill you. And I mean that literally."

His face took on the color of fresh snow.

I didn't have time to make good on my word, so I got into the back seat and told the driver to drive as fast as possible. "Siena, wake up." I ripped a piece of my shirt and tied it around her head to stop the bleeding. The bullet injured her scalp just above her ear. Her blood dripped everywhere, getting on the leather and the carpeted floors.

She was losing a lot of blood for just a graze.

"Fuck." I kept up the pressure and stared at her face, seeing her cheeks turn to milk. "Baby...stay with me."

———

I got her to the hospital and into a room instantly. The doctor arrived just seconds after we did and examined the wound in her skull. The hair in the area had to be shaved so the doctor could figure out what to do.

I stood off to the side, never so scared in my entire life. I rubbed my hands together and rested them against my lips, hoping that she would pull through this, that the wound was as minor as my brother described.

The doctor finally provided information. "The bullet scraped against her scalp. It moved past the bone but didn't pierce it. We'll give her a blood transfusion because she's lost so much, but she should be okay."

Thank fucking god. "Why isn't she awake?"

"Passing out is a natural defense to extreme trauma. It keeps the heart rate low and the blood pressure down. I'm sure she'll come around in a few hours. I'm gonna patch her up and get that transfusion going. Just sit tight."

———

I sat at her bedside and waited for her to wake up.

Gauze had been tied around her head, and an IV was placed in her hand. Her vitals were stable, so she would be okay.

But I wouldn't be.

My phone rang, and Bates's name appeared on the screen. My teeth clenched the second I looked at his name. My fingers ached to grasp a gun and pull the trigger. I wanted to execute him in front of my fountain like I did with all my other victims. I wanted to hang him from a noose and stab him in the gut.

I stepped outside and took it. "You have a lot of nerve."

"I just wanted to see if she was okay."

People passed me in the hallway but didn't stop me from raising my voice. "Are you fucking kidding me? You shot her in the head, and you want to see if she's okay? She's been shot in the head, asshole. Of course she's not okay."

"What did the doctors say?"

"She'll be fine. She's asleep right now."

"Good. I never meant to do any real damage—"

"Fuck. You." My brother had pissed me off a lot over the year, but never like this. "You stabbed me in the fucking back. You betrayed me. You're supposed to be the one person I trust most in this world, and now I can't trust you at all."

"We had to make it look real, Cato. We can't let Micah and Damien know how much she means to you."

I grabbed my hair and nearly yanked it out of my scalp. "Knock it off with that already!"

"And she needed to be punished for what she did. Let's not forget how much of a betrayal it was."

"We were supposed to scare her—not shoot her. You had no fucking right."

"I knew you wouldn't be able to do it."

"Because I'm not a psychopath!"

"I never meant to seriously hurt her—"

"Fuck off, Bates. If I see you again, I will kill you." I hung up and shoved my phone into my pocket.

When I returned to her bedside, she was awake. She stared at the monitor and examined her vitals as she tried to figure out where she was. When her eyes landed on me, they didn't have that deep look of affection I was used to. She tensed noticeably, pulling her IV with her as she prepared to defend herself. Her lips were pressed tightly together like she was prepared to scream, and the terror in her eyes showed her complete disgust.

"Baby—"

"Don't *baby* me. Don't ever *baby* me again."

Those simple words broke my heart. "Bates wasn't supposed to do that. That shouldn't have happened."

"But everything else was supposed to happen? I trusted you." Moisture flooded her eyes as she looked at me with a mixture of hatred and heartbreak. "I give birth to your daughter, and then you do this to me? I thought we were a team. But then you fucking stabbed me in the back like the piece of shit that you are."

"I was still upset about what happened. This gave me closure. It gave me justice. Now we can both move on."

"Justice?" she whispered. "Pretending to execute me is justice? For me trying to save my father's life? What about everything that's happened after that? What about Martina? Christmas? How many times have I told you I loved you without saying it back? I signed all that stupid paperwork to prove your money means nothing to me. I did all of that...but you really couldn't let it go?"

I held her gaze without any idea what to say.

"You somehow found a woman who loves you for you... and you do this to her?"

"You aren't so innocent—"

"We've come a long way since then. We're different people now—both of us. We have a little girl at home right now, and you thought it was appropriate to pull this stunt? Fuck you. Just...fuck you." She held up her hand and looked away, like my presence was too much for her.

I hated myself for how much I'd hurt her. I hated myself for being the cold and vicious man I was. "We're even now. We can move forward and start over—clean slate."

She gave a sarcastic laugh. "Let me shoot you in the head, and we'll be even."

"That wasn't supposed to happen. Bates shouldn't have done that—"

"And you trusted that hotheaded psychopath? I bet he's the one who talked you into doing it in the first place."

I didn't confirm it.

"Because the man I've been sleeping with wouldn't have done that on his own." She still wouldn't look at me.

"I will punish Bates for what he did. He won't get away with this."

"I couldn't care less about him. You're the one I care about, Cato. He's not in this relationship—you are." She crossed her arms over her chest and kept her gaze focused on the door.

"I'm going to kill him."

No reaction.

"I'm going to shoot him in front of the fountain."

"Is that how you solve all your problems?" she hissed. "Making them kneel and take a bullet to the brain? You already picked your brother over me, so there's no point in killing him. Whether he lives or dies makes no difference to me."

I stared at the side of her face and the white gauze that nearly matched her pearly skin. I could feel the hatred ripple out of her body in waves. All the love and affection I used to feel from her disappeared. I'd done terrible things to her in the past, but she'd somehow still loved me. But now...it seemed like I'd pushed her too far. "I'm sorry."

Her arms tightened over her chest. "Can I go? I need to get home and check on Martina."

Forcing a conversation when the wound was so fresh wouldn't change anything. She was livid with me and needed space. Maybe once she cooled down, she might listen to me. "I'll take you home now."

———

When we stepped out of the car, it was dawn. The sun rose over the horizon, and her blood was still visible on the ground. Drops of it had been left behind. She stopped and stared at it, like she was reliving that moment.

Then she marched into the house as quickly as she could, like she was trying to get away from me.

I let her get a head start.

I joined her in the baby's room upstairs. Siena sat in the rocking chair and breastfed Martina, rocking back and forth slowly as the sun filtered through the open window. I stared at her from the doorway, thinking about how beautiful she looked—how terrible I felt.

She looked up when she realized I was there. "Go away." She barely raised her voice as she addressed me. "Don't make me ask you again." She looked back at our daughter who was eating breakfast from her tits.

I wanted to stand there and watch her nourish our daughter because it was a beautiful sight. There was something so simple about it, so peaceful. But I knew I wasn't welcome—and I shouldn't be welcome.

I didn't know what else to do, so I went to my office to work.

10

SIENA

There were no words to describe what I was feeling.

Other than the pain I felt in my head, I felt pain everywhere else too—especially my heart.

I hadn't seen it coming because I trusted Cato so blindly. Even if he didn't say he loved me, I knew he loved me from the bottom of his heart. I knew he would never hurt me, never torture me.

But I was wrong about all of that.

Maybe he didn't love me.

Maybe I was just a stupid fool.

I moved some of my clothes and essentials back into my old bedroom while Cato was in his office. There was no way I would be sleeping next to him anymore. I used to hate sleeping in my bed alone, but now I preferred it over the man who'd betrayed me so violently.

I took Martina with me, and when it was time to go to bed, I changed her diaper, gave her dinner, and then put her in bed beside me. I placed pillows on the opposite end of the bed to replace Cato so she wouldn't roll over in her sleep.

We lay side by side, the two of us in our alliance.

Something about her brought me a sense of calm, made me feel like she would take care of me even though I was the one taking care of her. She had her father's eyes, but that didn't stop me from thinking she was the most beautiful thing in the world. I felt her fingers in between mine and watched her stare at me.

The door opened, and Cato stepped into the room, in just his sweatpants. He was ready for bed and must have figured out the two of us wouldn't be joining him. He stood in the doorway as he looked at us.

Martina cried the second she saw him.

"I just got her ready for bed." I rubbed her stomach to get her to calm down again.

"You didn't tell me you were moving."

"You didn't tell me you were going to torture me. Funny how things happen..."

He came to the side of the bed with all the pillows and moved them away so he could get close to Martina. "I'm here, sweetheart." His large hand squeezed her fingers gently. "Daddy's right here."

"You can stay until she falls asleep. But then I want you gone." I snuggled close to Martina and closed my eyes. I listened to her cries die away and her breathing slow down.

Cato didn't leave even when she fell asleep. "Baby—"

"You have no right to call me that. Please leave. I don't want to start this again when we just got her to fall asleep. So just go." I closed my eyes and waited for him to leave.

He didn't.

I opened my eyes again. "Cato."

"You like to sleep with me because I make you feel safe. Let me make you feel safe."

I released a sarcastic laugh. "The last time I felt safe was the day before I met you. And I haven't felt safe ever since."

———

A week passed, and we hardly spoke to one another.

I avoided him at all costs, sleeping in a different room and taking my meals after he left for work. It was a warm spring, so I took Martina on long walks in her stroller along the path in the backyard. I spent most of my time alone—with my daughter.

But that space only made me angrier.

I couldn't believe Cato did that to me.

My wound had healed enough that I didn't need to wear the ridiculous gauze around my skull. Thankfully, Bates hadn't appeared at the house because I'd probably have beaten him worse than he beat me. I was pissed at Bates for shooting me, but I was far angrier with Cato for putting me in that situation to begin with.

I'd thought we were past that nonsense.

I'd thought we had a deeper connection, a relationship that transcended words. I assumed he loved me as much as I loved him, but perhaps that was just a fool's enthusiasm. Now everything felt like a lie. He'd brought me back from France because he couldn't live without me, but maybe that was just an empty request as well.

I couldn't have meant much to him if he pulled a stunt like that.

Did that really give him any satisfaction?

I put Martina down for a nap in her crib then headed to his private gym for a workout. I'd started dieting the second I got home and exercising because I wanted to get back into shape, make everything tight again. I jogged on the treadmill for forty-five minutes before I moved to the free weights. I did a few basic exercises then wiped my brow with the towel because the sweat drenched my body. It felt good to work out hard, to push my body in ways it hadn't been pushed in a long time. It released all the toxins in my blood, made me have a goal that had nothing to do with Martina.

Earbuds played music in my ears, and I looked up to see Cato standing behind me in the mirror. He was in a gray suit with a black tie, looking like the billionaire who got off on terrifying everyone. His blue eyes were glued to mine, his gaze sometimes wandering over my workout outfit.

I pulled the cords out of my ears then returned the weights to the rack. "Martina is taking a nap in her crib."

"I know. I checked on her."

"Then why are you here?" I was so pissed off at him, I could be angry for an entire year. I had every right to move out of the house completely and return to my old place, but since Martina was so young, I knew I needed help from Giovanni and Cato. There was still so much to learn about raising a little girl.

"You know why I'm here." His hands moved into his pockets and he came closer to me, his eyes still watching mine in the mirror. Now that I could see both of us so clearly, I realized how much taller he was than me. I barely reached his shoulder. "I understand why you're angry with me. I understand why you won't talk to me. I get it...I do. But don't forget who I am. I never let betrayals go unpunished. I had to make you pay for what you did. No one gets an exception."

I rolled my eyes. "You're unbelievable. I just gave birth to your daughter, and you're trying to justify that... Pathetic."

"We're even."

"Didn't realize this was a game," I hissed. "I thought we were two people in a relationship. I thought we were two people who respected each other. Guess I was wrong."

"We are," he said. "But that relationship was built on a lie. I needed retribution."

"Congratulations, you got it. You only had to sacrifice our relationship to get it."

He tilted his gaze to look at the floor as he considered what I'd said. Even in a casual posture, his broad shoulders were undeniable. He was a powerhouse, an entire army wrapped up into a single man. "This relationship has been a mess since the beginning. We didn't get our shit together until recently. And Siena...I'm different now."

"You aren't different at all."

"I am," he said quickly. "And right now, I can promise you I would lay down my life for you in a heartbeat." He stepped closer to me, coming up behind me as he continued to hold my gaze. "I would do everything and anything to protect you. I would never, ever let anything bad ever happen to you or our daughter. If a gun were fired, I would take that bullet for you—even in my heart." His hands moved to my arms, and he rested his forehead against the back of my head. "I'm completely at your service. I promise, for the rest of my life, I will be exactly what you need. I will never lie to you, never hurt you, and I will always be loyal to you." He took a deep breath as he held me. "You said you would always love me...so please forgive me."

I stared at the ground as I felt the pulse in his hands. I was so livid just a few minutes ago, and now I could feel that rage slowly slipping away. It shouldn't matter that he apologized or said something so sweet. His actions were wrong —unforgivable. But my heart believed everything he'd just said, believed all the promises he'd just made. "I need more time to let it go."

He lifted his head and looked me in the eye in the mirror. "That's okay." His hands moved around my waist, and he tugged me close against him. His face moved into my neck, and he gently brushed his lips against my skin. "But you forgive me?"

I nodded.

He closed his eyes and released a quiet sigh. "Thank you." He released me. "I haven't dealt with Bates yet. What do you want me to do?"

"What does it matter what I want? He's your brother."

"Because I'll kill him if you want me to." Fearlessly, he looked into my gaze, telling me he would make good on his promise. He was my guard dog now, and whatever I asked for, he would deliver—even his brother's corpse.

"No."

"Then what do you want?" he asked. "He needs a punishment."

I didn't want to respond to violence with more violence. I wanted Bates to feel guilty for what he'd done, and the best way to do that was not to retaliate at all. He would have to live with his brother's disappointment for the rest of his life. That was good enough for me. "He can never hold my daughter again. Ever."

Cato gave no discernible reaction. He held my gaze, his blue eyes unemotional. He would serve out any punishment I sought, even if it was heartbreaking. Denying his brother the opportunity to hold his niece was far crueler than violence. "Alright. I'll make sure that never happens."

"Good. I should get back to my workout now..."

Cato obviously expected more from me because he sighed in disappointment. But he didn't make an argument for what he wanted, and he turned around and left the gym.

Maybe I shouldn't have forgiven him.

But it was impossible not to forgive the man I loved.

11

CATO

Night after night, I lay there alone.

It was the longest time I'd gone without sex, but that wasn't what bothered me most. I had no sexual appetite anyway.

All I wanted was Siena, in whatever capacity I could have her. Her hair used to brush across my chest when she moved in the middle of the night. Sometimes she spooned me from behind and gripped my waist. Sometimes she slept on me entirely. Now I slept alone—and my bedroom had never felt so cold.

I should wait until she was ready, but for a man like me, that was easier said than done. I was used to getting what I wanted by demand. I never had to work for a woman's affection or earn her forgiveness.

But that was because none of those women were real.

Siena hated me for who I was—but she somehow loved me too.

Her love was real. Her affection was real. And her love-making was real.

Fuck, I missed her.

She was down the hall in her old bedroom, my daughter with her. It was still early in the evening, so she was probably awake.

I'd considered stopping by for a visit, just to test the waters. I continued to give her the space she asked for to prove my sincerity, but as the days passed, the loneliness killed me. It seemed like I'd lost her all over again, like she was back in France, even though she was just down the hall.

When I couldn't fight it anymore, I threw back the covers and marched to her bedroom.

She sat up in bed reading a book while Martina slept beside her, wearing a blue onesie. She was sound asleep and not affected by the lamp on the bedside table. Siena lifted her gaze to look at me, and this time, I wasn't met with the same hostility. It was much dimmer now, like simmering coals of a dying fire. "Did you need something?"

"You." I approached the bed in my boxers and looked down at my daughter, who was even more beautiful when she was asleep. I spent time with Martina when I got home from work, but it wasn't the same as it was when the three of us were together. Even if we weren't talking, just being together was good enough.

She closed the book and rested it on her lap. "You know it'll be a few weeks before—"

"That's not what I mean. I just want you...I miss you." I went from being a playboy to a one-woman kind of man. Now my affection for this woman fueled my entire existence. While she was in another room, I could easily watch porn without her knowing about it. Or when I was at work, I could skip off and fuck someone else. Even if I could get away with any of those things, I never wanted to. This was the only woman I wanted. "I miss both of you."

"How am I supposed to fix that?"

"Let me sleep with you." I used to force her into her own bedroom because I didn't want to share my space—or my heart. But now I was used to having her beside me. I was used to that quiet breathing, her perfume, and knowing I was always there if she needed me.

She debated her answer silently, like she still wasn't ready to be what we were. It would take time to earn back her trust, if I ever did. It would take time to earn her affection. But I hoped I wouldn't have to earn back her love. "Alright."

It was the first time I'd had to beg a woman to sleep with me.

I moved to the other side of the bed and got under the covers, careful not to wake Martina. She was close to Siena, so I was able to slip into the bed without shifting the mattress too much.

Siena opened her book again.

I turned on my side and watched her read while Martina was oblivious to my presence. Now that I had these girls in my life, I truly understood how lonely I'd been before, how empty that existence had been. It was night after night of good sex, but the memory didn't last long before it was replaced by another. There was no substance to it, only bragging rights. "You were right about everything you said to me all those months ago... That's why I stayed. That's why the others faded away."

She kept her book on her stomach but turned to look at me.

"You looked past my image and saw all the emptiness behind it. When other people see success, money, sex, you see the truth—loneliness, despair, emptiness. You knew I had everything, but I also had nothing. I couldn't get angry about that because I knew you were right. You saw me for who I really was—and I was never the same."

She held my gaze, the emotion lingering under the surface.

"You made me a better man, Siena. It's taken a while for it to kick in...but you have."

A slight smile stretched over her lips as she closed the book she was reading. She set it on the nightstand and turned off the lamp before she got comfortable next to me, turning on her side so she could face me. "It's baby. Call me baby."

————

We weren't back to normal, but at least things were better than they were before. She moved her stuff back into my bedroom and resumed sleeping with me every night. She started to put Martina in her crib and listen to her cry for an hour without retrieving her.

Siena was strong.

"I hate listening to her cry," she whispered as the baby monitor kept projecting the sound of Martina's screams. "But she needs to get used to being alone."

"She's only a few weeks old..."

"The sooner, the better. Teaches her independence."

I didn't like it either, but I agreed it was the best parenting move. And it gave us the bed to ourselves. Sex was off the table until she healed, but that didn't mean we couldn't do other things. Right now, there was only one thing I wanted to do.

Kiss her.

I hiked her leg over my hip and moved my mouth close to hers. My mouth brushed her lips and I tested the waters first, to see if she would coldly reject me or warmly welcome me. I rubbed my nose along hers and pulled her tighter against me, wanting her to feel how aroused she made me. It didn't matter that her body had changed after carrying my baby, I wanted her as much as I had before.

When she didn't push me away, I kissed her.

Slow and easy, I moved my mouth with hers. I felt her lips with mine, sucked in her bottom lip with subtle aggression. Then I caressed her top lip with both my mouth and my tongue. I took my time because it'd been so long since I'd had this intimacy with her. I wanted slow down time and appreciate those pillows for lips.

I rolled her to her back and kept going, my hand digging into her hair. The heat cranked up almost instantly, setting us both on fire. I kissed her harder and deeper, my cock so hard it wanted to split in two.

I missed this.

I missed the passion, the chemistry.

I never had this kind of affection with anyone else, when I wanted to kiss a woman and never stop.

My hand moved between her legs, and I felt her clit through her panties. That little nub had been unavailable for so long. Now I circled it with my fingers, making her draw a sharp breath at the intensity. I wanted to slip my fingers inside her to feel her grow wet for me, but I steered clear of her healing flesh. I continued my kisses as I fondled her clit, breathing deeply into her mouth as I pushed her into a climax that made her hips buck. She rocked against my hand as she moaned into my mouth, her nails slicing me deeper than usual. It'd been just as long for her as it'd been for me, and she crumbled apart until she was a mess of sexual satisfaction.

Maybe she wouldn't be so mad at me anymore.

Just because we couldn't have sex didn't mean I couldn't make her toes curl.

When she finished every single aftershock of her pleasure, she rolled me to my back so she could do me next.

Yes.

Her mouth started at my balls, sucking and licking them, until she glided her tongue up my base. Over my vein like a bump in the road, she moved all the way to my tip then licked up the drop that formed there.

This was the best.

She lifted my big dick and shoved her throat over it, her mouth gaping open to accommodate me. Her flat tongue lubricated my shaft most of the way, at least, as far as she could go. She pulled up again, licked my tip, and then kept going.

It'd been weeks since my last orgasm. I didn't have any pride left to last a long time. I had nothing to prove to this woman. She knew exactly what I was capable of. My hand moved to the back of her neck, and I guided her over my length so I could come. "Here it comes, baby..." Like the good woman she was, she didn't gag. She took my load deep into her mouth and swallowed it like a pro.

I lay back and closed my eyes as I exploded, my body pulsating with happiness as I filled her mouth. The sensation spread from my fingertips to my toes. It was so good, making all my muscles tighten.

She licked everything away until my dick was as clean as it'd been when we started. She crawled up my body and held herself on top of me. "That was—"

I cupped her face and kissed her, not caring about the come in her mouth. I rolled her to her back and moved my fingers between her legs once again. Now that I had this connection again, I didn't want to lose it. I wanted to enjoy every second of it, to treasure this woman I'd taken for granted too many times.

————

I woke up earlier than Siena, so I changed Martina's diaper, gave her breakfast, and then spent some time with her over my own breakfast before I put her back in her crib for an early morning nap.

Then I went to work.

It àllowed Siena to sleep as long as possible before she spent the entire day with our baby. At least she was refreshed before she took up the task.

I headed to work then sat behind my desk in my office. Bates hadn't shown his face, only working with clients through emails and handling everything remotely. He knew what would happen if he crossed my path.

I was still livid with him.

Siena and I had finally found our way back to each other, but it was full of uncertainty and terror. I wasn't sure if she would ever fully forgive me. If the shooting hadn't happened, she still would have been angry, but not so pissed off. So Bates fucked that up for me—big-time.

Not to mention, he could have killed her. If his aim had been off just a little, she could be brain-dead right now.

To my surprise, Bates stepped into the doorway. Dressed in a fresh suit like he was ready for a day at the office, he stared at me hesitantly, like I might pull a gun out of the drawer and shoot him in the head.

It was tempting.

Bates continued to watch me, trying to assess my mood.

I leaned back in my chair and opened the top right drawer. Inside was a blade, a blade perfectly designed to slit someone's throat. I shut the drawer, pulled it out of the sheath, and then played with it between my fingers.

Bates didn't cross the threshold into my office. "So you're still mad, then?"

"You tell me."

He glanced at the knife. "Yeah...I think so."

"You're stupid to show up here."

"I was hoping you'd had enough time to cool down."

"Cool down?" I asked incredulously. "You shot my woman. You could have killed the mother of my child."

"I was never going to kill her."

"It was dark. Sometimes the hand slips."

"My hand doesn't slip, and you know that."

I spun the knife between my fingers. "You seem confused. Not killing her isn't the issue. Shooting her in the first place is the issue."

"And I apologized—"

"Which means nothing."

"What if I apologized to her?"

I scoffed. "She doesn't care enough to hear your apology."

"Then what can I do, Cato? I know it was a dick thing to do, and I'm sorry. I don't have a legitimate justification."

"No, you don't." I tossed the knife on the desk. "It took me weeks to get her to speak to me again. Weeks to get back into her bed. Weeks to get her to kiss me. She would have forgiven me if we'd done things my way, but I almost lost her because of you."

"She would never leave you. Loves you too much."

"And you'd shoot the woman who loves your brother?"

"She still needed to be punished—"

"I will decide how to punish my woman. Not you. This isn't the fucking bank. There are no joint decisions when it comes to my private life. You had no right to overstep your boundary like that. I'll never forgive you for it."

It was the first time he seemed genuinely heartbroken. "Cato...come on."

"Come on, what?" I hissed. "I asked her what she wanted me to do about you. I told her I would kill you if that's what she wanted. Whatever vengeance she wants, I'll honor. You know what she said?"

His skin started to fade to the color of paper.

"She said she never wants you to hold our daughter. Ever."

Instead of being relieved by that sentence, he seemed heartbroken again.

"Do you understand me?"

"I would never hurt—"

"That's not why. You've lost your rights as an uncle. She's stripped away your title, and I'll honor it."

"I think I would rather be shot..."

"I'm not done." I held up a finger. "That was her justice. I have my own."

He leaned against the doorway, prepared for whatever sentence I would hand down.

"One day, you're going to meet the woman you can't live without. And when that day comes...she will pay the price."

He started to breathe harder, like the sentence had struck a chord. "You don't think that's a little unreasonable?"

"Not in the slightest." I held his gaze without blinking.

"But she's innocent. Siena—"

"Was punished for her crime. You took it further than necessary. I will hurt your woman the way you hurt mine. And I promise you, I will keep my word."

"Good thing I'm not into monogamy..."

"For now. But trust me, she'll walk into your life when you least expect it. I'll be waiting for that moment, Bates. When I see that affection in your eyes, that devotion that's written all over my face every day, I will fulfill my promise."

"Couldn't you just kill me instead?"

I smiled, getting the exact reaction I wanted. "No. That would be too easy."

"Siena doesn't seem like someone who would approve this."

"Because she doesn't know—and you aren't going to tell her." He'd betrayed me once. He'd be stupid to do it again.

He didn't argue with me, but he was clearly disgruntled. "Then where do we stand?"

"We'll never be the same again. But I won't stab you—if that's what you're worried about."

"No, I don't care if you stab me." He walked farther into the room and approached my desk. "You aren't just my brother, Cato. You're my..." He couldn't say the rest out loud. "I can't lose you. I need you. And I don't mean for the business. I mean...you're the most important person in my life. I love you..." He dropped his gaze as he turned emotional. "I'm sorry for what I did. Really. Truly."

I was eternally grateful when Siena forgave me, especially when I couldn't have blamed her if she'd never forgiven me. I felt like I should extend that mercy to him, but what he did was unforgivable. "I've never felt so terrible in my life. When I saw her hit the ground...I felt like I'd lost everything."

"I know..."

My eyes watered just thinking about that moment, that moment when I thought the bullet pierced her brain and ended her life. In that split second, it made me realize that all the money in my account meant absolutely nothing. All the success I'd found was laughable. My greatest accomplishment was finding that woman. "Bates, I love her."

His eyes softened as he took a deep breath. "I know, man."

"I love her more than anything in the world—even you. What I feel..." My hands balled into fists as I tried to describe the sensation. "It's happiness. And it's the first time in my life I've ever actually felt it. All the women before her were just practice. They were just ways to kill time until the right woman walked into my life. Now that I have her, I feel complete. And when I thought that was gone...I was gone."

Bates listened to every word. "Have you told her?"

I shook my head. "I'm too much of a pussy."

"You could have told her to get her to forgive you."

I shook my head. "That's not how I wanted to say it. I didn't want her to think I was only saying it to get her back. That would be cheap—and make it less meaningful."

"Then call her and tell her."

"I'm not doing it over the phone. I'll do it when the time is right."

"Well, she already knows, so I guess it doesn't matter."

After what I'd done, maybe she didn't believe it anymore. "I hope so."

After a long pause, Bates sat in the leather armchair. "How's Martina?"

"Wonderful."

"Really? She doesn't cry and shit all the time?"

"Are you trying to get on my good side?" I asked sarcastically.

"You know what I mean. Being a father can't be easy."

It was a drastic change from how my life used to be, but I did enjoy having her around. I had to change my priorities and work out in the evenings since I needed to take care of her in the morning, but being a parent was about making sacrifices. "It's a lot easier than I thought it would be. I guess it's because she's my daughter...so I don't mind taking care of her. And I have it easy. Siena is the one who takes care of her all day while I'm at work."

Bates nodded. "Do you want to have more kids?"

"As many as she wants to have." She'd told me she wanted to marry me and make more babies with me, even before Martina had arrived. Now that I'd admitted my feelings to myself, I knew that was exactly what I wanted.

"It's crazy to think that just a year ago you were the asshole playboy who only believed in threesomes."

"Yeah...it is." I was a different man until that woman walked into my life and told me off. I got her pregnant by mistake, but Martina ended up being the greatest thing that ever happened to me. Without her, I would have killed Siena that day...and never would have what I had now.

"But you're happy...so I'm happy for you."

"Took you long enough."

He shrugged. "I'm a little slow. But you already knew that."

———

I had to work late that night. My clients flew in from China, but their flight got delayed for bad weather, so I had to stick around for a few extra hours.

When Siena got worried, she called. "Hey, you're usually home by now..." She didn't outright ask for an explanation, probably because she didn't want to seem jealous like she'd been in the past.

I liked it when she got jealous, so I didn't care. "I had a meeting that got pushed back. Bad weather delayed their flight. I just finished with them, and I'm going to be heading home soon."

"Good. It's dark already." It was almost summer, so the days were getting longer. It seemed like just yesterday when winter made the sun go down by five.

"Yeah, I know. How's our little girl?"

"She's good," she said, her tone picking up noticeably. "Just gave her dinner and a bath. Now she's in her pajamas and ready to see her father before she goes to sleep."

"I can't wait to see my girls."

"We can't wait to see you."

I stayed on the phone with her, tempted to tell her how I felt. Thinking about both of them at home waiting for me made my heart burst in my chest. I didn't miss the bars, the booze, or the boobs of my former life. The only thing I ever missed was my family waiting for me at home. But I didn't tell her the truth, wanting to make sure I looked her in the eye when I told her how I felt. "I'll see you when I get home."

"Alright."

I waited for her to hang up before I walked out of my office and left the building. My car was waiting for me, so I got in the back seat and stared out the tinted window as we drove through the city and headed to the countryside. Three cars were in the front and three were in the back, protecting me everywhere I went. If someone wanted to take me down, they would have a hard time doing it.

When the car reached the countryside, a large explosion nearly broke my eardrums. My instinct was to duck and get out of view of the windows. Bright light filled the sky in all directions, billowing flames reaching into the darkness. Even inside the car, I could feel the heat from the fire.

Shit.

I reached under the seat and grabbed the loaded pistol. "What the fuck is going on?"

The driver called for backup, and I sat up to look around. All the cars in my entourage had exploded. Some were still on fire, and others had rolled off the road and into the grass. It was safe to say all the men were dead. Their cars had been loaded with explosives and timed to go off at this particular moment.

That meant the war with Micah and Damien wasn't over.

I only had time for one phone call, and as much as I wanted to tell Siena I loved her before I was killed, I had to call Bates.

Thankfully, he answered right away. "Are you still at the office—"

"Someone took a shot at me. All the cars in my fleet have been destroyed by explosives. I'm still in the car, but I know more are coming. No idea who's behind this. I'm three miles outside of Florence."

Bates didn't ask any questions. He switched into survival mode. "I'll round up the other guys now to intercept you. Stay on the—"

A tank came out of the darkness and slammed into my car.

My seat belt was off because I'd removed it to duck on the floor. My body went flying with the momentum, slamming into the side as the car rolled from the blow. I was pushed off the road, rolling continuously and hitting my head on every surface. The phone kept flying. "Bates, if you can hear me, I've been hit by a tank." The phone probably broke on impact.

The car finally came to a stop, and I was disoriented. The spinning and the collision had nearly broken me in half. My head beat like a drum, and my wrist felt injured. My gun was on the floor, so I grabbed it and prepared for anything.

The front door opened, and a man took out the two men in the front seat.

Fuck, I was next.

I was the last one alive on purpose. They didn't want me dead right away, not until they got what they wanted. They would torture me until they broke me. The gun in my hand shouldn't be used for defense, but suicide. Why suffer when I could just end it now?

But then I thought of Siena and Martina.

I couldn't give up—not yet.

The back door opened, and Damien poked his head inside. "Mr. Marino, beautiful night, isn't it?" His eyes gleamed with mirth, like he'd been counting down the days until this moment arrived.

I shouldn't have shot him in the shoulder. I should have shot him in the head. "I've seen better."

"Awfully arrogant for the last man standing."

"Just because my men are dead doesn't mean I'm alone. And so much for that truce, huh?"

"It was a stupid move on your part...and all for pussy."

My fists wanted to pummel his face, but I had to keep my cool. I had to pretend Siena meant nothing to me—otherwise, they might use her against me.

"I've been wanting to fuck that cunt for a while. So I understand your fascination."

It took all my strength to do nothing. "Do you always talk this much?"

"When I'm in a good mood. Now, get out." He stepped back so I could climb out of the car. I left my gun behind because there was no point in bringing it along. Once I stepped out of the car, it would be taken from me. Hopefully, Bates was still on the line and had heard that conversation. Even if he didn't, he would figure out who took me. He'd been suspicious of Damien for months.

I stepped out of the car and brushed off my suit like I still had all the power in the situation. "What now? Dinner? Movie?"

Damien chuckled. "You know what's next—and you aren't going to like it."

I was returned to Florence and their headquarters. I kept looking out the window hoping my men would show up and take me back, but they never managed to intercept me. I knew my brother was doing everything possible to get me back, but once I was inside their fortress, it would be impossible to get me out.

Unless he used nuclear weapons.

That would just defeat the purpose.

Their fortress was new on the outside, but ancient below. It went deep under the surface, making them impenetrable by invasion. Once they got me under the hatch and deep underground, I knew I would stay there until I became a corpse.

I wasn't scared of death.

I was scared of what would happen to my girls.

Bates would take care of them, I believed that.

But I wanted to be the one to take care of them.

I was taken underground and into a cell made entirely of concrete. There was a small bed in the corner, a chair, and a toilet, so they obviously expected me to last through their interrogation for a few days.

Fuck, how did this happen?

They'd had to wire the cars somehow. That couldn't have been easy. It was genius—and that pissed me off.

"Sit." Damien nodded to the metal chair in the corner.

I took off my jacket and placed it over the chair, retaining as much power as I could. Showing fear would only make it worse. Regardless of what they did to me, I wouldn't cave. I wouldn't give them any satisfaction. "I should have some time."

"Yeah?" Damien asked. "How thoughtful of you."

"I won't give you what you want. You'll torture me until I crack, but I won't crack. You'll contact Bates next and offer my freedom in exchange for his cooperation. He won't give you what you want either. So I suggest you kill me."

"Or maybe I need to crank up my torturing methods right from the beginning." He stood in front of me, his arms crossed over his chest. "When a man hasn't felt a needle in his eye or a hot iron in his ass, he thinks he can handle anything. But once it really gets rough, he breaks. Trust me, they all break. You'll be no different."

12

SIENA

Every time I called, it went straight to voice mail.

Something wasn't right.

He should have been home an hour ago.

My heart was beating so hard.

Giovanni came into my room without knocking. "Bates is outside. He's gathering all the men. Something's wrong."

I almost ran out of the room, but then I remembered I had a daughter I couldn't leave unattended. "Giovanni—"

"I'll take care of her. Go."

I ran down the stairs then made my way outside. The last car left the roundabout as every single man under Cato's payroll took off—and left the house unprotected. "What's going on?" I found Bates standing there on the phone, talking to someone about his mom. He hung up and turned to me. "Damien has Cato. He called me when it happened. They ambushed him, and there's nothing he could have done about it."

"Oh my god..." I covered my mouth with my hands as the tears emerged. "No. No. No."

"I sent the rest of the men to intercept him, but I have a feeling they've already made it to their headquarters by now."

I paced in a circle, my hands digging into my hair. "So what? Break down the front door and get in there."

"It's not that simple—"

"I don't care if it's simple! Get in there and get him out."

"Listen to me." He grabbed both of my shoulders and shook me. "I want my brother back as much as you do, but their headquarters is underneath the building, deep underground. I can crash the building down, but that would only trap Cato underneath it. We could storm inside, but the hatch can't be broken."

"So we do nothing?" I shrieked.

"No...I just have to figure something out."

"What do they want from Cato?"

"Everything."

"What does that mean?" she hissed.

"They want access to all his bank accounts, all of his assets, all of his billions."

"Then give it to them."

Bates gave me a disappointed look. "We agreed we would never give any of that up."

"So you'd rather die for money?" I asked incredulously. "Is it really more important than your life? Your brother's life?"

"It's not just about money. It's about power. It's about not handing over everything we worked for to some assholes. We don't negotiate with assholes. Cato and I both agreed that if either one of us were captured, we wouldn't negotiate."

"He must feel differently now. He didn't have us when he said that."

Bates shook his head. "Trust me, he won't change his mind. He would rather die than let them win."

"No!"

"It's not about money—"

"Money has done nothing but ruined your lives. Don't you see that?" Tears streamed down my face. "Just give them what they want. Get Cato back... I need him. His daughter needs him."

He gripped my shoulders and tried to calm me. "I will do everything I can to get him back, okay? Look, I'm on your side. I just need a second to think."

"We don't have a second." I pushed his arms down. "They're going to torture him. They're going to torture and kill him the way they tortured and killed my father. I'm not letting that happen to him."

"Well, do you have any ideas? You've been there before. How do we infiltrate their building? Get underground?"

I'd been there before, but never under the hatch. "I've only been on the bottom floor. I didn't even know they had an underground. I don't see why we can't storm the building, kill all the men, and smoke them out."

"I'm sure they're prepared for that eventuality."

"Then negotiating is our only option."

"I can't, Siena—"

"Then offer them something. Offer them a billion or something."

He shook his head. "Then all our enemies will think they can do that to us."

"How about we just focus on getting Cato back before we think about the future?" I hissed. "Give them the business and get out of the game for good. Money isn't worth this nightmare."

Bates sighed. "Siena, you're oversimplifying it."

"This is your brother. He'll be tortured and—"

"I may not be in tears, but that doesn't mean I'm not falling apart," he growled. "I love my brother more than anything in this damn world. I want him back more than you do. But it's not that simple. If we get out of the game, people might hunt us down and slaughter us anyway. This is beyond your understanding at the moment."

Bates was just talking in circles, and we weren't finding a solution. Damien was taking pleasure in this because he knew Cato was sleeping with me. So this was personal to him. He would make it hurt for that reason alone.

The thought of Damien gave me an idea. It made me sick to my stomach, terrified, and so scared that my hands actually shook...but it was the only solution that might actually work. I didn't care what the consequences would be to me. All I cared about was getting Cato out of there...because he didn't deserve that fate. "I have an idea...and I know it'll work."

"What?" Bates asked, stepping closer to me in enthusiasm. "What is it?"

"Damien wants me…"

He raised an eyebrow. "What's that supposed to mean?"

"I could walk in there and offer a trade. Cato for me. He'll take it."

Bates looked furious, like I'd just suggested we forget about Cato entirely. "Cato would rather die than let that happen."

"I know…but I don't care."

"I can't let that happen, Siena. I prefer him over you, but he would kill me if I didn't stop you. Cato would rather be tortured a million times than let you take his place."

"I wouldn't be taking his place, necessarily."

He cocked his head. "You're gonna let a guy rape you until he kills you. That's worse than death, if you ask me."

"But it's not worse than Cato dying. This is the only option we have. I walk in there, make the trade, and then…I'll find a way out."

"You don't understand how complicated that is. I don't have a schematic for you. I can't give you a blueprint."

"I'll memorize the way out on the way in."

He dragged his hands down his face. "How are you going to get away from Damien in the first place?"

"He'll take me somewhere private to fuck me. That's when I'll pull out a knife hidden in my hair and kill him with it."

His nostrils flared as he sighed. "What if you offer the trade, and they keep you without letting Cato go?"

"I'll offer my compliance—and that will make it worth his while."

"But he can get billions out of Cato. You're just pussy...sorry."

With Cato captured, I didn't have time to be offended. "You've seen how distracted men can become over pussy." Cato changed his whole life when he met me, and Damien had wanted me for years. "Trust me, Damien wants me. He'll make the trade."

"Fuck, I don't know..."

"You'll wait for me outside in a shitty car. I'll run out and hop in...and we'll drive like hell."

He stared at me for a long time, his blue eyes shifting back and forth as he looked into mine. His jaw was clenched tight as he considered my offer. "What about Martina?"

"Giovanni will take care of her...and give her to Landon if Cato and I don't survive." I didn't want to think about not seeing my baby again. That terrified me even more than losing Cato. But one day she would understand why I had to do this...because I had to save the man I loved.

He closed his eyes and sighed. "Are you sure about this?"

"Yes," I said without hesitation.

"There's a very strong possibility you might not get out."

"And if that happens, Cato won't stop until he figures out a way to get me back."

"But you would have to live with...you know."

Being raped. Every day. For who knows how long. "I would much rather suffer that than let Cato be tortured—a million times over. Sex is just sex. I'll close my eyes and think about my daughter. I'll trick Damien into becoming infatuated with me so he'll treat me well. And then maybe I can find my own escape. All I know is...doing nothing isn't an option. I can't leave Cato there."

He still grappled with this heavy burden. If he let me go and I didn't escape, Cato would never forgive him. His phone rang at that moment, and he answered without looking at the screen. "You didn't make it?" he asked. "Alright. Head back." He hung up.

I already knew what security had told him.

He lifted his gaze and looked at me again. "I'm sorry I ever doubted you, Siena."

———

Saying goodbye to my daughter was the hardest thing I'd ever had to do.

I held her close to my chest and rocked her back and forth, feeling her warmth in my arms. She smelled like baby shampoo and laundry detergent. I ran my fingers over her small hands, and I kissed each one, wanting to treasure how she felt before I left—possibly for good. "Martina, I love you so much." I kissed her forehead. "But I love your father too...and I have to save him. He'll be home soon, and he'll take care of you." Tears fell down my cheeks as I gripped her tightly, unable to say goodbye to the most important thing in my life.

Giovanni cried too, knowing how hard this was for me. "I'll take care of her, Miss Siena. Don't worry."

I handed her back to Giovanni and cried harder. "Tell Cato I love him."

"Of course, Miss Siena." He wrapped his arm around me and hugged me. "You're a smart and strong woman. If anyone can make it out of there, it's you."

"Thank you. I'll remember that..." I looked at my daughter one last time before I turned away and walked out of the house. Tears kept falling down my cheeks as I got into the passenger's seat of the car.

Bates looked at me from behind the steering wheel. "You're absolutely sure you want to do this?"

I couldn't live with myself if I left Cato to suffer. It would haunt me every single day. I knew he was suffering that very moment, and the longer I waited, the weaker he became. Even if they didn't kill him right away, the injuries themselves might. "Yes."

Bates hit the gas, and we left the estate.

———

The drive to Florence seemed to last a lifetime.

We didn't speak the entire way.

There was nothing to say, not when we were both thinking about Cato at the exact same time.

We entered the city and drove through the streets until we approached their building. Like always, it was dark and seemed abandoned. They hid in plain sight, which made them more difficult to target.

Bates pulled up to the curb. "I have a few men who will pick up Cato when he steps outside. I'll wait for you here since this car isn't conspicuous. This is your last chance, Siena. I strongly discourage you from doing this."

"No matter how small the odds are, I have to try." I looked into his eyes, seeing the genuine concern on his face. "I love him so much. I can't even describe it. I would give up my life for his in a heartbeat. There's no fear. There's no hesitation. Regardless of what Damien does to me, I'll be relieved Cato is free."

He sighed. "If this doesn't work, Cato and I will figure out a way to get you back. And if that means Cato has to give up everything...I'm sure he'll do it."

"I know he will."

He continued to look at me, the emotion written all over his face. "I'm sorry for what I did. I'm sorry for not believing you. I'm sorry...for everything. You're the greatest thing that's ever happened to my brother."

"You were just trying to protect him."

"But there was nothing to protect him from." He rested his hand on mine. "Good luck." He gave me a gentle squeeze before he pulled his hand away.

I opened the door and prepared to step out. "I forgive you, Bates." I shut the door behind me and walked around the corner to the secret entrance. I'd passed through it before, and I did the same procedure now.

The camera examined my features, recognized me, and allowed me to step inside.

Two men armed with rifles studied me. The one on the left spoke. "Siena Russo, why are you here?"

"To have a word with Damien." Now that I was in the lair of the demons, there was no time to be scared or emotional. I had to be hard and cold if I was going to survive down here. "He's not expecting me, but he'll be happy to see me." I stepped forward and allowed the men to move their metal detectors across my body. As I expected, they didn't check my bun.

That was a good sign.

One of them stepped off to the side to radio down into the hatch.

I waited patiently, seeing the guard look me up and down like I was a piece of meat.

I glanced at him, my gaze hostile. "Do you mind?"

He grinned and looked away.

The other guard returned. "He'll see you. Come with me." He took me by the arm.

I yanked my elbow out of his grasp. "I'm not a blind dog. I can see where I'm doing."

He didn't try to push me again. He took me farther into the room and down a few hallways until we entered a room with an enormous hatch in the floor. He went to a keypad and typed in a code.

I managed to catch a glimpse.

34892

Easy enough to remember.

The large door slid open, revealing a spiral stairwell that went deep underground. There were lights along the walls for illumination.

Jesus, this place was nuclear-proof.

The guard guided me to the stairs and followed behind me. At the top of the stairs, I noticed a similar pad where the code could be entered to exit. I remembered what it was before I made the descent. It seemed to take fifteen minutes before we reached the bottom and stepped inside a large room. It didn't seem like we were hundreds of feet underground, but in another building just like the ones on the surface.

The guard escorted me again, taking me down a few hall-ways until we entered a row of cells.

I memorized all the turns.

My heart started to beat harder the closer we came. All the cells looked like prison cells, and I suspected I was about to see Cato. I just hoped I could keep my emotions together, to not burst into tears at the sight of him. Whether he was injured or unharmed, it would be difficult for me to seem indifferent. The fact that I was making this gesture at all was proof that I loved him, but I didn't want to wear my heart on my sleeve to Damien.

The guard knocked on the door before he stepped inside. "Here she is." He gave me a push.

I stepped inside, and the sight I saw nearly made me burst into tears. Cato was on the ground, naked with the exception of his boxers, and he was so bloody that his features were barely distinguishable. He was breathing, but he seemed so weak...like he couldn't even stand.

I fought the tears as hard as I could.

Damien smiled at me like this was the happiest day of his life. "Wow, you don't look like you just had a baby." He looked me up and down with approval.

I tried not to stare at Cato, who seemed to be unconscious. "I hit the gym pretty hard."

"It shows." On the table beside him was a bloody hammer. I hated to think what he'd done with that.

I was so glad I'd come. Whatever Damien did to me would be worth it to get Cato out of there.

"So, what brings you here?" Damien asked. "You missed the best part of the show." He looked down at Cato. "He lasted longer than I thought he would. But unfortunately... we're just getting started."

Cato shifted from his spot on the floor. He moved slightly, like he was coming back around.

I had to get him out of here. "I'll make this quick. I'm looking for a trade—him for me."

He grinned. "No offense, honey. But he's worth billions. You're worth nothing."

"I'm worth more than billions. You would know if you'd ever had me."

His smile dropped.

"Make the trade. I will cooperate fully. I will be whatever you want me to be. And I'm sure Cato will pay you whatever you want to let me go...so it's a win-win for you." That was an offer he couldn't refuse.

He examined me with new eyes. "You were supposed to bring him to us. But now you're sacrificing your life for his. Ironic, isn't it?"

Cato started to wake up more, his breathing escalating.

"I suppose," I said. "Do we have a deal or not?"

Damien looked me up and down as he considered it. "I have wanted to fuck you for a long time. I thought my interest would fade once the baby came, but I guess not. You clean up good."

"Thank you," I said with sarcasm. "Let him go, and I'll do whatever you want."

"Siena Russo, obedient?" he asked, his head cocked. "Didn't think that was possible."

"It is possible. You'll see for yourself once you let him go."

Cato pushed his body up so he could lean against the wall. His face was so bloody that his blue eyes were striking against the redness that dripped down his face. He must have thought I was a hallucination at first because he didn't react right away. But then he realized his mind wasn't playing tricks on him. "Siena?"

"Yes," Damien said. "She's come to take your place. Isn't that sweet?"

Cato yanked on the chains that kept him against the wall and tried to break free. "No! Siena, no!" His strength came out of nowhere, and he rose to his feet, using all of his power to try to break the concrete wall that bound him. "No! Don't do this! No!"

I couldn't watch him. It was just too painful. "Let him go. When I know he's outside, I'm all yours."

He yanked on the chains again. "I would rather die! Siena! No!"

Tears burned behind my eyes, but I didn't let them fall. "Cato, it's alright."

"It's not fucking alright." Cato gave me a fierce look of despair mixed with betrayal. "No. I would rather bleed to death than let him have you. No. Let me die here, Siena. Let me die here."

I kept my eyes on Damien. "Do it."

Damien whistled, so the guards came in. "Take him to the surface. I want proof that he's free. I'm sure Siena won't be cooperative until she knows for certain her man has been released."

Cato went berserk. He fought the guards and the chains and behaved like a man who hadn't been beaten bloody. His strength came from somewhere deep within, deep in his heart. "Siena!"

I stepped aside and let him pass. I couldn't make eye contact with him, not when he was this furious, this heart-broken. I knew how much it killed him to leave me behind, to know what Damien was about to do to me.

They finally pulled him out of the cell, but I could hear him fight the entire way. His yells echoed down the hall. Even when he moved upstairs, he continued to fight like a bull that couldn't be tamed.

I did the best I could to keep my emotions in check, to stay calm. Watching them drag Cato away was one of the most difficult things I'd ever had to do, but looking at the bloody hammer in the corner told me I'd made the right decision. If I'd waited until morning, he might not have been able to walk.

Damien didn't waste any time. He shut the cell door and stripped off his clothes. First, his shirt, and then everything else. He shed every single piece until he was completely naked, his dick hard and ready to take me. He lay back on the bed with his hands behind his head. "How should I fuck you for the first time? Hmm…"

I stayed in the same spot I'd been before, waiting for any indication Cato was actually free. The clothes he wore when he entered this place were gone. All he had were the boxers that hugged his waist.

I hated to think about how much he had suffered. Made me sick to my stomach.

"This is the best plan," Damien said. "I get to fuck you. And then Cato will hand over everything to save you.

Good thinking, sweetheart. You've always been too smart for your own good."

No matter how smart I was, I always seemed to get into these situations. "How will you know when he's been released?"

"The guards will send the security feed to my phone."

I sighed as I continued to wait, wanting Cato to be free as soon as possible. He needed to get to a hospital right away. Even his chest and back were coated with blood. He probably had broken ribs and internal bleeding.

Twenty minutes later, Damien finally got the video sent to his phone. "Here you go, sweetheart." He tossed the phone at me.

I hit play and watched the feed. They pushed Cato out of the building and onto the sidewalk. He could barely stand because he was so weak, probably because he fought the entire way to the surface. One of his cars pulled up, and his men helped him inside. Then they took off.

He was free.

"I'm a man of my word. Are you a woman of yours?"

I set the phone on the table and turned to him. "Yes."

"Then drop the clothes." He sat up on the cot with his legs hanging over the edge and his feet on the ground.

It disgusted me to drop my clothes and let him see me naked. But if I didn't cooperate, that would be a dead give-away. I took my time as I peeled off every inch of clothing, stalling as long as possible until I was just in my thong.

Damien's dick was rock hard. "You're beautiful. No stretch marks. But your pussy might not be as tight as what I'm used to. So maybe we'll start with an ass-fuck. But first...I want you on your knees...your mouth on my dick."

I couldn't wait to kill this asshole. I couldn't wait to avenge Cato. I couldn't wait to get justice for my father.

I pulled my panties down my legs then moved to my knees like he asked.

"Grab my dick, sweetheart. See what a man feels like."

I complied, disgusted at the feeling of his pulse against my fingertips. His size was pathetic in comparison to Cato's. "How do you like it?"

He grinned. "I like this version of you. The wetter, the better. I feel like I just bought the sexiest whore from the Underground." His cock twitched in my hands, like he was getting off on his own words.

Egotistical freak.

I spat on his dick first and smeared my saliva up and down his base. Instead of being disgusted by what I was doing, I focused on the move I was about to make. I had to calm him, to make him drop his guard so he wouldn't be able to stop me. I jerked him from tip to base, making his thighs tighten and his eyes close.

He leaned back on his elbows as his breathing escalated. "I'm so glad you fell in love with Cato Marino. Who knew it would be the greatest thing that ever happened to me?"

"And the greatest thing that ever happened to me." I subtly pulled the knife from my hair then while he breathed through the pleasure. Then I pressed the blade against his shaft and severed it from his body—like the cold-hearted bitch that I was. "That's for Cato." Blood squirted everywhere, and he let out a scream.

I covered his mouth with my hand and pushed him against the cot, doing my best to stifle his screams. With an injury like that, he wouldn't last long before he died. It was a horrific way to go, but after seeing Cato beaten so badly that he was hardly recognizable, I felt no remorse.

I smashed his face into the cot while he got blood all over the bedding. His severed dick was somewhere on the floor, probably shriveled up and lifeless by now. I tuned out the sounds of his cries and used my strength to anchor the pillow over his face, to wait until the fight ended and he passed on to the next life—in hell.

Finally, his jerks slowed down, and he gave up. His lungs screamed for air they wouldn't receive. His heart slowly stopped as blood no longer flowed. After a few seconds, he turned motionless, but he also became rigid, all the muscles in his body tightening at his moment of death.

Damien was gone.

Good fucking riddance.

I covered him with the blankets then put my clothes back on. Thankfully, the blood was on my skin so it was easy to hide underneath my shirt and pants. All I had was the small knife I'd just castrated him with, so I searched the room for a gun. Damien's clothes had nothing useful inside of them, and since the cell was solid concrete, there wasn't a place to hide a weapon anyway.

I could see all the blood from Cato's body on the floor.

But I couldn't think about that right now.

I knew he would be proud of me for what I'd just done, for taking my fate into my own hands. I got revenge for my father. I got revenge for Cato. And I got revenge for myself. Now all I had to do was sneak out of here.

I tucked the knife into my palm and moved down the hallway. I'd memorized the route during the walk, repeating the directions over and over in my mind so I wouldn't forget them. But now I had to mirror those moves since I was going in the opposite direction—and completely flip them. I was starting at the end and going backward. But all

I needed to do was get to the stairway with the hatch. The rest of the way would be easier.

Every time I came to a corner, I stopped and peered down the hallway to make sure no one was coming. I moved as quietly as possible down the hallways, and unfortunately, a lot of them looked identical.

That wasn't good.

I stopped in front of a sign mounted on the wall and realized it was a map. It showed the location of the main stairwell out to the hatch.

Well, that worked out.

I kept walking, but I had to stop when a guard was about to cross my path. He moved down the hallway with a pistol sitting on his hip. Dressed in all black, he looked the same as the others guards I'd come across.

I wondered how long I had before someone discovered Damien's body.

They would sound the alarm and lock the hatch. Then I would be stuck down here until they found me.

Micah would torture me until he killed me.

I waited for the guard to round the corner, and I thought about my little girl. I had to make it back to her no matter what. My daughter shouldn't grow up without a mother.

I'd lost my mother in adulthood, and I would never recover from it. She was the light of my life, my best friend. Martina needed me...and so did Cato.

I had to make it out of here.

The guard rounded the corner and reacted quickly when he noticed me. His eyebrows almost jumped off his face, he opened his mouth to yell, and he reached for his gun.

I punched him in the face, kicked him in the balls, and then stabbed him in the throat.

He crumpled to the ground—dead instantly.

There was nowhere for me to hide his body, so now I had to hurry. I took his pistol and moved faster, taking less caution at being noticed because I was running out of time. There were probably cameras around here, and now that the guard's corpse lay in the middle of the hallway, I only had a few minutes to get out of there. The pistol wouldn't be enough to keep me safe.

I finally made it to the big stairwell. It had taken us fifteen minutes to come down it earlier, so it would take me just as long to make it back to the surface. I put the pistol in the back of my jeans and started to run, knowing I was racing against the clock. There was probably a system override they could use to lock me inside. Then I would be trapped at the top of the stairwell with nowhere to run.

I ran as fast as I could, as quickly as my heart would allow. I'd been working out every day, but I was seriously out of shape. I gripped the rail to pull myself up as I moved, and within five minutes, I was panting hard and slick with sweat.

But I didn't stop—because I had a little girl waiting for me.

I started to hear a commotion down below, an echo of voices that carried all the way to my position. "Shit." I sprinted faster, running in spirals as I moved to the surface. I passed two lights at every interval, and I glanced up to see how close I was to the top. "Just a little more." I kicked it into overdrive, knowing Cato would be furious with me if I got this close but didn't cross the finish line.

I got to the keypad and stared at it blankly.

Shit, what was the password?

That ten-minute run had knocked me out, and I could barely think straight. Memorizing the path had been my priority, so I had shoved this to the back burner. I couldn't randomly hit numbers because that would probably initiate a lockdown sequence.

Think.

Thirty seconds later, it finally came to me.

34892

I typed the numbers into the keypad, and then the door started to slide open.

Thank god.

Slowly, it moved, revealing the ground above. Once a crack opened wide enough for me to fit through, I climbed up and got to my feet.

There was a guard standing there, staring at me like he couldn't figure out if I was supposed to be there or not. He finally made the right call and drew his weapon.

I shot first.

He fell to the floor with a thud.

The gunshot was loud in the enclosure, so the other men must have heard it.

I didn't have time to creep around.

I sprinted like hell, moving through the main room and back to the secret doorway. I knew the way because I'd been there before. But now the trick was not getting shot. Men chased me with their weapons drawn.

If I didn't stay ahead of them, I would be pumped full of bullets.

I made it to the front door and shot both men before they could react, each in the head. Then I pushed through the double doors and made it outside. It was still dark, but it was nearly dawn.

I sprinted to the meeting place where Bates would be sitting in the old car.

His eyes widened in shock when he saw me, like he'd never actually expected me to get out of there alive.

"Go!"

He started the engine and pushed the passenger door open.

Before I even made it all the way inside, he hit the gas.

I jumped in and shut the door as we took off at full speed.

Men poured out of the building and onto the sidewalk with their guns raised. A lot of them fired at us, breaking the back windows and destroying the taillights, but once there was enough distance between us, we were finally out of firing range.

Bates drove sporadically through the streets, speeding as he made sharp turns. Both hands were on the wheel as he got us out of the city and into the countryside. Once we were on a straight road, he gave me the most incredulous look I'd ever seen. "I can't believe you did that."

I still hadn't caught my breath. Sweat dripped from my forehead and into my eyes. I tried to wipe it away with my hand, but it was no use. There was sweat everywhere. "Neither can I." I chopped off a man's dick and killed a few others. I'd turned into a killing machine, something I didn't know I was capable of. But when it came to my family...I was willing to do anything to protect them.

And I wasn't ashamed of that.

13

CATO

So much fucking pain.

Everything was broken. Everything screamed. It was the kind of agony that made you wish for death.

But it was nothing compared to watching Siena take my place.

That was the most painful thing I'd ever had to do.

To watch her hand herself over to that asshole so I could go free.

I would rather die a million times.

But there was nothing I could do. I fought the guards until they threw me on the sidewalk and my men carried me away.

Now I was at my estate, barely able to stand as I stepped into my home.

"Mr. Marino?" Giovanni caught me before I slammed into the ground. "What are you doing here? We need to get you to a hospital."

"Martina? Where is she?"

"She's in the kitchen, perfectly safe."

I'd already lost one of my girls. I wasn't going to lose another. "Siena took my place...I have to get her back." I slowly slid to the floor, too weak to even hold myself up.

"Sir." Giovanni used his strength to guide me carefully to the floor. "We have to get you to a hospital."

"Siena!"

"Sir, if you die, who will take care of Martina?"

All I cared about was saving Siena, even if it killed me. But I forgot about the person who mattered more, the person I swore to protect above all else. If I died, she would be alone.

"You need to go to the hospital, Mr. Marino."

"I..." I could barely think, I was so weak.

The door burst open, and Bates walked inside. "Cato! Shit." He leaned down and looked at me. "Jesus Christ, you look dead."

"Siena..." I tried to get up again, but I couldn't.

"She's right here," Bates said. "She's right here."

"What?" I asked, barely keeping my eyes open.

"Oh my god..." Her voice resonated in my ears, so beautiful it seemed unreal. "Cato..." She moved over me and cupped my face. "You need to get to a hospital. Now."

"Siena?" I grabbed her wrist, wanting to feel her pulse, wanting to feel that she was real. "You're here."

"Yes, I'm here. I got away."

I brought her hand to my lips and kissed it. "Thank god." My breathing turned deeper and heavier as I became weaker. I'd never felt this weak in my life, never felt so powerless. Somehow, Siena managed to get us both out of there without my help.

"Bates, we have to get him to a hospital," Siena said. "He's barely holding on."

"We'll take the chopper," Bates said. "We can all fit."

"What about Martina?" she asked. "Can we put a car seat in there?"

"I don't fucking know," Bates hissed. "But Damien's men are only a few minutes behind us. That chopper is our only chance to get out of here." He turned back to me. "I know it hurts, Cato. But you have to walk to the chopper. I'll get you to the hospital as soon as I can, but we need to hurry."

I knew it would be painful, but I had to keep moving. I had to get Siena and Martina out of there. "Alright...let's go." I pushed to my feet then hooked one arm over Giovanni's shoulder. Siena supported my other arm and took some of my weight on her slender shoulders.

Bates grabbed Martina's carrier. "Let's move."

————

"Stay awake." Siena gently slapped my cheek.

My eyes opened again, and I saw Bates flying the chopper. I had no idea how much time had passed. It seemed like hours, but it could only have been minutes. My eyes closed once more, and I felt myself drift away.

"Come on, Cato." Siena slapped me again. "Look at Martina."

I peered down into her face, seeing the little headset covering her ears. She stared at me with fascination, like this chopper ride was fun. I started to slump forward as the weakness overtook me.

Giovanni grabbed me and pushed me back. "How much farther?"

Bates spoke over the radio. "Almost there."

———

We landed on the roof of a hospital. Personnel came out with a gurney to wheel me away.

All I could think about were Siena and Martina. "What about them?" I asked my brother over the radio.

Bates shut down the helicopter and pulled off his headset. "Don't worry about them. I'll take care of them." He grabbed my arm and helped me out of the chopper so I could get on the gurney.

The second my back hit the support, I grabbed my brother by the arm. "If I die, I need you to take care of them, alright?"

"You know I will."

"I mean it. They're your responsibility. I want Siena to have all my assets. Everything. Give it to her."

"You have my word. But that's not gonna happen." He kissed me on the forehead. "I'll see you soon."

14

SIENA

They wheeled him away and took him inside the hospital.

I didn't say goodbye because there wasn't time. He'd needed medical attention hours ago. Every moment he waited hurt his odds of surviving. So I let him go without a kiss because he already knew I loved him.

I'd proved it a million times over.

"What now?" I held Martina against my chest as we stood on the rooftop of a hospital in London. We'd had to touch down to refuel once along the way, but Bates insisted this hospital was our best option. The London Eye was across the river, visible as the sun rose and struck it with its brilliance. It was my first time in the city, but I didn't have the opportunity to enjoy it.

"I have an apartment here. You guys will stay there and lay low." Bates pulled back his sleeve and looked at the time. "I'll escort you there and come back to the hospital."

"Why can't we stay here too?"

"The hospital is no place for a baby without an immune system," Bates said. "And if Micah's men are as furious as I think they are, they're going to keep looking for Cato. I've got to keep you hidden. And I've got to stay here and protect Cato." He must have seen the concerned look on my face because he added, "You've done everything you can. Now you need to take care of Martina. Let me handle Cato."

I felt wrong leaving Cato there. I wanted to be there when he woke up, for him to see my face and know everything was okay. "Call me when any little thing comes up. I mean it. I want to know everything."

"I know. Now let's get off this roof."

———

Bates had a nice apartment in north London, an apartment that bigger than a lot of houses. It had bullet-proof windows, a large kitchen, a big living room, and plenty of space for the three of us. "I bought this place under one of my shell corporations. It's possible to trace it back to me, but it would take some time. You should be safe here. There are guns on the top shelves of all the closets if you need any." He turned to Giovanni. "Get some groceries, baby food, diapers, and whatever else Siena needs. I'll check in when there's something to report."

Giovanni nodded then left the apartment.

I stood in the room alone, holding my daughter as the darkness started to overtake me.

Bates stepped closer to me, looking at me with new eyes. "Are you okay?"

"We don't need to worry about me right now..." All I could think about was Cato, the strongest man in the world reduced to a pile of broken bones. "When I walked into the cell, he was on the ground...covered in blood. There was a bloody hammer on the table." My eyes watered at the memory. "If I'd gotten there any later...he probably wouldn't have hands." A tear escaped and rolled down my cheek.

Bates wore an agonized expression, the idea of his brother in pain hurting him too.

"When they took Cato away, Damien wanted me to suck his dick. I started jerking him off, and when he closed his eyes, I cut off his dick."

Bates's eyes widened, his mouth gaping open in shock.

"I smothered him with a pillow until he died."

"Jesus Christ."

"I shot a few men on the way out. I'm not even sure how I escaped... I just got lucky."

"No. You're a determined badass. That's how you got out, Siena. You saved my brother's life."

"I don't feel bad for what I did. But that memory of Cato on the ground will haunt me forever."

"I know..."

"So, no, I'm not okay. I won't be okay until Cato is okay."

"He'll pull through this. I know he will."

"He better." Tears broke the surface of my eyes and streamed down my cheeks.

Bates moved in to hug me, but then he stepped back like he thought that was a bad idea. "This is a nightmare for all of us...a memory that won't fade easily. But Cato will be alright. Micah will be pissed and try to annihilate us, but that's a good thing because they'll be easy to take out in the open. We'll gather all our allies and destroy them once and for all."

"Why would they challenge you if they're outnumbered?"

"Because they thought they could take Cato, get me to cooperate, and wipe us out. But since their plan didn't work, they have to kill us off now. So, they'll be looking for

Cato. They'll know he's in the UK because the healthcare is the best here. But it'll still be difficult to pinpoint his location."

"Couldn't they see he's been checked in to a hospital?"

"He's under a fake name."

"Oh...that's good."

"Cato asked me to take care of you while he's indisposed. So, you're going to have to listen to me for a while...even though you probably don't want to. I need you to stay here and don't draw any attention to yourself." He fished in his pocket and pulled out a phone. "Call me if you need anything."

"Okay." I took the phone and slipped it into my pocket.

He stared at me for a while, like there was more he wanted to say. "You have bigger balls than I do, Siena. No one else would have the strength to go down there and do what you did."

"Love makes you brave. Love makes you feel like you can do anything...because you have too much to lose. Even if that had turned out differently, I still would have done it. Seeing Cato like that...I never want to see him like that again."

"Hopefully, you don't have to." He stepped away. "I'll call you when I know something."

"Alright." I watched him walk out the door and leave us alone in the living room. I stood with Martina in my arms, the only comfort I had after the horrible things I'd just experienced. I felt like I was stuck in a nightmare. I couldn't wake myself up, and I was subjected to the horror indefinitely.

I looked down at my daughter. "Daddy is going to be okay...we'll have him back in no time."

15

CATO

My eyes were closed, but I felt my consciousness rise. I heard my brother talking on the phone.

"Claw, Micah took out a hit on Cato. We managed to get out of there, but Cato is too injured to fight. I need you guys to help us take out Micah once and for all." He sat at my bedside, keeping his voice low.

Claw was audible over the phone. "You want our help?" he asked, somewhat comically.

"He took out most of our men. When we draw them out into the open, we need your assistance wiping them out for good. I know you have all the weapons to make it happen—since I paid for them."

Claw responded, "Just because you gave us a couple loans doesn't mean we owe you. You have to make it worth my while. The loans are eradicated."

Bates chuckled into the phone. "So you basically want eight hundred million for your trouble?"

"Depends. How much do you want to get rid of Micah?"

Bates considered the question for a while. "I'll cut the total loan in half. Four hundred million. Same interest rate on the reduced amount. Take it or leave it."

Claw didn't hesitate. "We have a deal. Call me when you're ready."

Bates hung up.

I opened my eyes and stared at the ceiling. It took a moment for my eyes to focus. Everything slowly came into view, the white walls of the hospital room and the monitor to my left.

The first thing I thought about was Siena.

I sat up to look for her.

Bates grabbed my shoulder and pushed me back down. "She's at my apartment in the city with Giovanni. Perfectly safe."

"Why isn't she here?" I asked in a raspy voice.

"I thought she would be safer somewhere else. Micah is probably hunting you down as we speak."

That was true. Siena had escaped and made him look like an idiot. He wouldn't be happy about that. "She's okay?"

"Perfectly okay."

"Martina?"

"She's with her." He patted my arm. "You're going to be here for a few days. They had to give you a few blood transfusions because you lost a third of your own blood. You have internal bleeding, a few broken ribs, and fractures in your arms. But good news is, you should be okay."

I didn't feel okay. I felt pain everywhere. "What the fuck happened, Bates? Why the hell did Siena take my place like that? You better not have been a part of that."

He lowered his gaze and didn't make eye contact with me.

"If I weren't so weak, I would kill you right now."

"I tried to talk her out of it, I swear. But she was going to do it with or without my help, so I decided to help her."

I shook my head and felt the pain throbbing in my body. "You helped my woman get raped to save my life?"

"She was never raped, Cato. She got out of there before anything happened. That was the plan all along."

That took away all the pain inside my chest. I feared my woman had been pinned down by another man, that he'd taken advantage of her when he had no right. I would rather die than let that happen. I would have taken that hammer to the ribs a million times rather than accept that fate. "How did she escape?"

"She killed Damien."

My head turned his way, shocked by what I heard. "With her bare hands?"

"No. She had a knife hidden in her hair. He took off all his clothes as he prepared to...you know. He sat on the bed with his hard dick hanging out, and that's when Siena cut it off. She smothered him with a pillow as he bled to death."

I smiled through the pain, so proud of what he'd said. "That's my baby..."

"Then she snuck out of the hatch and back to the surface. She had to kill a few men on the way, but she made it outside without a scratch. I picked her up and headed back to the house."

Siena saved my life and kicked ass in the process. She got revenge for what Damien did to her, did to me, and did to her father. She saved both of us without having to give herself up. I never would have wanted her to risk herself in the first place...but at least everything turned out well. "No one else would have done that for me. Any other woman would just go through my stuff and take everything they could find while I was being tortured to death. You were wrong about her, Bates. So fucking wrong."

"Yeah...I realize that."

Now I missed her even more. And I felt guilty for subjecting her to that ridiculous torment. I never should have put her on her knees and scared her like that. It was stupid, and I wished I could take it back. "I want to see her."

"I think it's best she stays where she is. When you're better, we'll stop by the apartment, and you can see both of them."

"Then give me your phone." I extended my hand.

He called Siena before he handed it to me and stepped out of the room.

Siena answered right away, Martina crying in the background. "What do you know?"

I treasured the terror in her voice, the way she audibly cared for me. "It's me."

She turned silent, Martina still continuing to cry. Then Siena started to cry too, her quiet tears making it over the line. Her emotion flowed through the phone, heavy and heartbreaking. Every time she tried to silence herself, she just cried harder.

I let her get it out, let her bare her soul to me. "It's okay, baby. I'm okay." Listening to her cry elicited my own tears...but I didn't let them carry over the phone. I let the moisture build up in my eyes, making my vision slightly blurry.

"Thank god..." She sniffed.

Martina stopped crying.

"I was so worried. I couldn't sleep...I couldn't eat."

"Well, when we get off the phone, you should do those things. You need to rest. You need to eat."

"Okay..."

"Martina needs you to be strong for her."

"I know..."

I listened to her quiet sniffles slowly fade away. "Bates said I'll be here for a few days. After that, we'll head home."

"You're going to be okay?"

"Just a few scratches and bruises."

"Cato."

I sighed into the phone. "I lost a lot of blood. Broke some ribs. Have fractures in my arms. I'm in bad shape, but it won't kill me. It'll be a while before I recover."

She sighed in relief. "Good...I'm glad you'll be okay. I've been so worried."

"I know. The worst is over."

"Yes..." She sighed into the phone, her pain still audible.

I wanted to tell her how I felt, to tell her that I loved her from the bottom of my heart. But I didn't want to do it over the phone. That was why I wanted her to visit me, so I could have the opportunity to do this right. "Bates told me you killed Damien."

"Yeah...I did."

"You're one hell of a woman."

She stayed quiet.

"I'm not happy you did that...but I'm proud of you for pulling it off."

"I don't care if you're mad at me, Cato. I would have done it a million times. I wasn't going to let you stay down there. I knew if I didn't get away, you would find a way to rescue me."

While being Damien's plaything in the meantime. "You cut off his dick?"

"Right at the base."

"That's my baby."

"I'm glad he's gone. It was such a relief to watch him die... to know he couldn't bother us ever again. I needed revenge for what he did to you. Seeing you so weak...it broke my heart. It broke my heart more than losing my mother or my father. This was a whole new kind of pain...I can't even describe it."

"I know."

"It was so hard leaving Martina behind, but I knew I had to do it. If I didn't come back, she would understand one day."

She would understand her mother sacrificed herself to save her father. What could be more romantic than that? "It's over now, so we don't need to worry about it anymore."

"I'll feel better when I see your face...when I can touch you."

"Me too."

"What do we do when you're released from the hospital?"

There was only one thing on the agenda. "We return to Tuscany and finish this."

"Take out Micah and the rest?"

"Yes. We'll work with our allies to bring him down. Now, we've declared war. Only there won't be two sides. It'll only be us annihilating them. Micah will go into his bunker for a while where we can't get to him. But when he comes out, which he will, we'll hit him hard. Then it'll be over for good."

"I can't wait until that moment comes. We can finally be free."

"Yes." I would make sure nothing happened to the three of us ever again. I would annihilate my enemies, and they would know not to mess with me again. I was an enemy you didn't want to have. "How's our girl?"

"She's very fussy. We're in a new place, and her father isn't here. I think she's just uncomfortable."

"I'll see her soon."

"She knows. She knows you love her too."

She wasn't the only one I loved. "You feel safe there with Giovanni? I can send Bates to you."

"No, we're fine. We're just counting the moments until you're out of there."

I wanted to stay on the phone with her forever, but Bates walked back into the room. "I'll talk to you soon."

"Alright. Bye."

I hung up and returned the phone.

"How is she?" Bates asked.

"Better now that she knows I'm okay."

"Good. I know she's eager to see you."

"I'm eager to see her too." As much as I wanted her here with me, I preferred to keep her safe. I was the target, not her. So, as long as she wasn't near me, nothing should happen to her.

"How's Martina?"

"Siena says she's fussy."

"Probably misses you."

"I know she does," I whispered.

Bates leaned back in the chair and relaxed. "Claw is on board with us. Said he'll help us destroy Micah if we only make him pay back half of the loans."

"That's fine." I didn't care about money right now. I didn't care about pride. I just wanted Micah to be gone in whatever way possible. "I don't care."

"So, when we're ready, I'll call him. I figured we would return to Tuscany and decide what to do then."

"I wonder if my house is still standing."

Bates shrugged. "The security team was still on site."

"Or they were there..."

"I haven't checked in."

"What about Mother?"

"I got her out of there hours ago. The guys took her to Greece. I talked to her a while ago, and she's fine. She's worried about you. And Siena had me alert Landon to go into hiding."

Everyone who mattered seemed to be safe and sound. "That could have been a lot worse."

"Yeah, I agree."

"I'm sorry I didn't listen to you." Bates warned me that something was wrong, but I brushed it off. We could have taken care of this much sooner if I'd just valued his opinion.

"It's okay. I shot your woman. We're both idiots."

"Yeah...I guess we are."

Bates looked at the clock on the wall then turned back to me. "It's getting late. You should get some sleep."

"You don't have to stay here with me, Bates."

"Yes, I do. If an asshole walks through that door, I'm prepared. So just relax. I got your back."

———

Days later, the doctor finally discharged me from the hospital.

My vitals had improved, and I was given pain medication for the road. I was stable, but I still hadn't returned to my former strength. It would take me a long time to get back to where I used to be. My broken ribs would take the longest to heal—and they caused me the most pain.

I walked on my own two feet as I left the hospital and got into the car Bates brought to the entrance. I sat down in the passenger seat and then we drove through the streets. It took me a few seconds to figure out where we were. I knew we were in the UK, but I didn't know exactly where. "London?"

"Yes."

"One of my favorite cities."

"Maybe the three of you can enjoy it another time." Bates drove to the apartment and parked in the underground parking garage. We rode the elevator to his floor then stepped inside the apartment.

Siena clearly hadn't been expecting me, judging by the shock on her face. She was on the floor with Martina, who lay on a blanket playing with some colorful toys. Tears sparkled in Siena's eyes instantly, and she got up so quickly she almost fell forward. She righted herself and came to me, the tears freely streaming down her cheeks. "You're out..." Her arms opened to hug me, but then she changed her mind and grabbed my wrists instead. "I don't want to hurt you..."

"This doesn't hurt." My hand slid into her hair as I kissed her in the living room. My fingers felt the soft strands that I had gotten used to touching every single day of my life. I kissed her slowly on the lips, taking my time as I appreciated this woman's love. Our mouths moved together slowly, and my heart ached for the sacrifices she'd made for me. I might be dead right now if it weren't for her.

Her tears rolled over our mouths, but that didn't stop her from continuing the kiss. She kept her hands on my wrists and refrained from touching my chest or my stomach. She was delicate with me when she used to be hard. "Cato, I love you. I love you so much."

I rested my forehead against hers and didn't hold back. I'd never wanted to tell her the truth for fear of what it would do to me. I couldn't share my power. I couldn't trust her. But now I knew I could trust her more than anyone else in the world. So I told her the truth...something I should have said a long time ago. "I love you too, baby. More than anything in this world."

She pulled away so she could look into my eyes and see the emotion that matched hers. "Cato..."

"I'm sorry I didn't say it sooner."

"You didn't have to... I always knew."

———

My private jet picked us up in London then took us back to Florence.

I experienced pain pretty much every moment of my existence now, even with the painkillers, but I tried to seem normal in front of Siena. She was heartbroken at the sight of me, and I didn't want her to feel worse than she already did. She carried my pain the way I carried hers. When they'd dragged me away so she could give herself to Damien, my mind had snapped. She must have felt the same way when she saw me on the ground, weak like a corpse.

She sat beside me in the seat with Martina in her arms.

Martina was wrapped up in a blanket with her head supported by her mother. She looked up at me with the same fascination as always, like she knew exactly who I was. She didn't understand what a father even was, but somehow, she knew I loved her and protected her. She was the greatest thing that had ever happened to me.

"Do you want to hold her?" Siena asked.

I would love to, but I was too weak. I'd have to use my core to hold her in my arms, and even the slight strain was extremely painful. "I would love to, but I think it'll be a while before I can."

"Of course..." She continued to keep Martina close. "Is the pain still bothering you?"

"A little," I lied. "But looking at her makes me forget about all that."

"Good. When I was in the apartment alone, she made me feel so much better. You weren't there, but I felt like I still had a piece of you."

"I know what you mean." I rested my hand on her thigh, grateful I had these two back in my life. I'd almost lost them, and they'd almost lost me.

Bates walked over. "Can I talk to Cato for a second?"

"Sure." She unbuckled her safety belt and moved to a different seat.

I was angry the second she was gone. She was the light of my life, and whenever I couldn't see her, the world suddenly felt dark. "What's up?"

"Micah has disappeared again. He's either gone into hiding, or he's under the hatch."

"He can't stay there for long." I wasn't concerned about it. He was like a rat in the sewer. If he didn't want to drown, he'd have to come up for air. "I'd like to kill him now, but I can be patient. The second he makes his move, we'll take him out."

Bates nodded. "If he's smart, he'll leave the country."

"Doesn't matter. He could go all the way to the Arctic, and we would still find him. He knows he's a dead man. He's just too much of a coward to face that truth. Not yet, anyway."

"You're right," he said in agreement. "The security team said the house is fine. Micah's men came to the gates but quickly realized we weren't there."

"How?"

"They must have seen the chopper in the sky."

That thing saved my life and my home. "So the place is intact?"

"Security said they left right away. There was a shootout, of course, but nothing to write home about. And you don't need to worry about them hitting you there because they're underground."

I looked forward to sleeping in my own bed, to being surrounded by the walls that kept us safe.

"I'll let you know if anything new pops up." Bates left the seat and moved into the rear of the plane.

Siena returned to the seat beside me. "Everything okay?"

"Micah is underground. We'll have to wait a while until he pops his head up."

"He can't stay like that forever. Even if he does, he's practically imprisoning himself."

"I agree. He'll come out to play soon."

She rested Martina in the crook of her arm and crossed her legs. "Bates said he was wrong about me."

"It's so obvious, he had to say it."

"He apologized and said I was a badass."

"Also obvious..."

She rested her head against the back of the chair and looked at me. "It seemed like he meant it. So I forgave him."

"For shooting you in the head?" I asked incredulously. "That's not something you forgive someone for."

"By that logic, I shouldn't forgive you for marching me outside and making me think you were really going to shoot me." She looked at me with victory in her eyes, knowing her argument was sound.

It was irrefutable. "And maybe you shouldn't forgive me either..."

"I already have, and I don't regret it. I don't regret forgiving him either. He and I are on good terms now."

"Because you pulled off an incredible stunt. He was forced to admire you, to respect you."

"And that's created a new relationship. So maybe we should let the past go and move on. Not letting him hold Martina seems a bit cruel."

"He was pretty bummed when I told him."

"Then I can't enforce that. He was just trying to protect you...and I understand that."

Maybe she could forgive him for what he did, but I couldn't. I would make good on my word someday. When he found the woman he loved, I would hurt her the way he'd hurt Siena. It was only fair. "I'm not ready to forgive him so easily, but I'm glad you are."

"He sat at your hospital bed for four days."

"And I would have done the same for him even if I was pissed at him. Doesn't change anything."

"What about—"

"This is between him and me, baby. If and when I'm ready to forgive him, I will. Until that time comes, let it go."

She turned back to Martina and turned quiet. "Alright."

I just got Siena back into my life, and I didn't want to start it on bad terms. "I'm sorry. I didn't mean—"

"Let's just forget it. We're almost home, and I'm excited to be back. I miss my bed. I miss the way the hardwood smells. I miss the way the sheets feel against my skin. I miss us... I miss being together."

————

I was relieved to see the estate in perfect shape. The gates hadn't been breached, and the landscaping was exactly the same. We pulled up to the front of the house then stepped inside, surrounded by the sturdy walls of this fortress.

I moved slower than I normally did because my broken ribs inhibited almost all of my movements. Just a subtle turn was enough to make me writhe in pain. The doctor said it would take time for all the bones to heal so I should be patient.

Bates walked in with me. "I've already started hiring more security. It'll take a while to get everything back in order, but for now, we still have half our men. That should be good enough for the time being. I doubt Micah will storm the gates, but if he does, we'll be ready for him."

"And the Skull Kings will be here in no time."

"With eight hundred million in weapons."

The house wasn't quite as spotless as it used to be since Giovanni hadn't been there to keep it in perfect condition. But now that he was back, he would restore it to its former glory.

"You want me to stay?" Bates asked. "Need me to do anything else?"

At a time like this, it was probably best if we stayed together. He had his own men at his property, but anytime we were apart, we were vulnerable. If he were captured, we'd have to do this whole thing all over again. "Stay. Pick whatever room you want."

"Can I bring a guest?" He waggled his eyebrows.

My only response was a glare.

He shrugged. "It was worth a try. I'll grab my stuff and return in an hour."

"Hurry."

"You worried about me?" he asked with a smile. "Good to know you don't hate me anymore."

"Who said I didn't?"

He winked then walked out.

I looked at the three stories of stairs with dread. I used to be a strong man who could carry Siena all the way to the very top—and now I could barely carry myself. My body didn't feel the same anymore. It was broken and aged behind repair. That hammer did immense damage to my frame, and I bit my tongue a few times when I refused to scream.

Siena stopped at the foot of the stairs. "There are rooms on the bottom floor, Cato."

Now I looked weak in front of her—and I hated that. "I'll be fine." I sucked it up and walked all the way to the top floor, stifling the pain as best I could. Now that I was up there, I wouldn't be returning to the entryway unless it was an emergency. No reason to put my body through that torment again.

Siena put Martina in the crib before she helped me undress in our bedroom. She peeled my shirt off gently, doing her best not to react to the scars and stitches. As much as she tried to fight it, the emotion was impossible to deny when it danced across her face like that. She took care of my jeans next then helped me into bed.

I sat up against the pillows and felt my entire body ache. Never in my life had I felt this terrible. Good thing the doctor was generous with the pain medication.

Siena sat at my side and ran her fingers through my hair. "I'll take care of you. Whatever you need, I'm here."

"I should be the one taking care of you..." I looked into her green eyes and treasured the sight. I could have lost her for good, and it would have haunted me every single second until I got her back. This woman had proved her love a million times, and I was too stupid to see it. Now I couldn't unsee it.

"You will—one day." She smiled at me as she continued to run her fingers through my short hair. "We'll take turns taking care of each other. Then when we're a hundred, Martina will take care of us."

"And our other kids."

Her hand stilled at my words, her eyes crinkling at the corners in emotion. "Our other kids?"

"You said you want two kids, right?"

"Yes. But do you?"

I nodded. "Maybe more than two."

She released a deep laugh, her eyes sparkling in happiness. "Ambitious."

"You know me, baby. I'm a very ambitious man."

"Well, let's get you better first. So that's step one."

"I want to make another baby as soon as you're ready."

"Two babies in diapers...that sounds like a handful."

I shrugged. "Nothing we can't handle. And if it is too much, we can make Giovanni take care of them."

She laughed. "Poor Giovanni. We dump everything on that sweet man."

"That's what I pay him for." I smiled as I looked at her, the woman who sacrificed herself to save me. The only other woman who would have done that was my mother. I didn't want Siena to do that, but her loyalty touched me. Loyalty had always been important to me, along with trust. She'd earned both those things. "I'm sorry...for everything."

"You have nothing to be sorry about, Cato." She grabbed my hand and held it on her thigh.

"You were right. I was too scared to tell you how I really felt. I was a coward."

"Coward is a strong word."

"And it suits me." I squeezed her hand. "You've had so much power over me since the beginning, and I hated that. Then when you tricked me...I felt foolish. I felt stupid and foolish. I was afraid to give you that power again."

"Understandable."

"But a real man shouldn't be a coward. A real man should wear his heart on his sleeve. I'm sorry I didn't do that sooner."

Her eyes softened with emotion. "I always knew, Cato. So there's no need to apologize. I saw it in the way you looked at me, the way you took care of me, the way you made love to me. You wore your heart on your sleeve...even if you didn't realize it."

16

SIENA

Six weeks had come and gone, and Cato had improved significantly. He had the strength to move around again. He didn't hit the gym or exert himself too much, but he was able to shower on his own and stand for long periods of time.

Even though he felt better, I forced him to stay in bed.

"Baby, I'm fine—"

"Stay." I placed the sheets over his lap.

He rolled his eyes. "Come on—"

"No. Just because you're feeling better doesn't mean you should run around. You could reinjure yourself and make it a million times worse. So you're going to stay in bed until you're completely healed." I placed Martina in bed beside him with her favorite colored plastic keys to play with. "And you have your daughter for company."

"As much as I enjoy hanging out with her, I have other things to do."

"Yes," I said in agreement. "Like get better."

He sighed under his breath.

"I'm gonna go get you some lunch. Keep an eye on her."

"You're just trying to make me feel useful."

"You are useful." I leaned down and kissed him. "Take advantage of this time you have with her. Before you know it, she's going to be all grown up."

"Don't talk like that," he said coldly. "I want her to stay like this forever."

"I don't," I said with a laugh. "My nipples are raw because she sucks on them so much."

"Even when she stops, they're still going to be raw." He gave me a playful look.

I left the bedroom and headed downstairs, trying to forget that last comment. Six weeks of convalescence was a long time to go without much action. Sometimes we kissed and touched each other in bed, but it'd been so long since we'd actually made love. It'd been about three months.

I missed it so much.

I went downstairs and found Bates in the conference room. He'd pretty much moved in to the space since he lived in the house with us. He handled the business remotely, rarely going to the office in Florence. "I'm gonna get some lunch for Cato. You want anything?"

"A salad is fine." He finished typing on his laptop then looked up to meet my gaze. "How is he?"

"Restless. Annoyed. Eager."

"Can't blame him."

"I'm having him watch Martina so he has something to do."

"He goes from running the biggest bank in Europe to watching a baby... Anticlimactic."

"At least it gives him something to do." I stepped farther into the office. "No sign of Micah?"

He shook his head. "Still underground. He hasn't fled to another country. My men have been watching the building, and the only thing that goes in and out are supply trucks. So I suspect he's willing to live underground long enough for us to forget about him...not that we ever could."

"That's cowardly." To live deep underground to avoid a fight that he started in the first place was pathetic. What kind of life could he have down there anyway? There was no sunlight. Just women and booze.

"I'm sure he's comfortable. It's better than death, I'll admit."

"Maybe we should lure him out. Bait him."

"And how do we do that?" he asked. "The only way that would work is if he thought he couldn't lose."

Bates and I talked about the bank, the estate, and Micah almost every day. I seemed to replace Cato as his sounding board for ideas and solutions. The past really seemed to be a distant memory now that we'd established this cama-raderie. It was hard to believe he pointed that gun at my head and pulled the trigger. "Then make him think he can't lose. We can pretend Cato passed away from his injuries. Micah will think you're alone and grieving. When he comes out to take you down, that's when you take him out."

Bates stared at me blankly as he considered it, going over my idea in his mind. "Cato would never go for it."

"Why not?"

"He's too stubborn to let people think something so small killed him. He would also think it's cowardly."

"Well, it was cowardly for them to break the truce Cato offered them."

He shrugged. "True..."

"Unless you want to storm the hatch. I got down there before. I might be able to do it again."

"They'll have changed the code by now—at least a dozen times."

"It's still possible to get down there. I'm sure he has women visit him all the time. I could slip in there—"

"You're really going to put Cato through that again?" he asked incredulously. "I'm not on board with that. Cato and I are finally on good terms, and I'm not going to screw that up so soon."

"It's still a good idea. Get one person in there to get the hatch open. Then the rest of the team moves in, takes out all the men on the bottom floor, and then we go underground and hunt down Micah. Sounds like a good plan to me. I know the area better than either one of you. It makes sense that it should be me."

"Not gonna happen."

"And they'll never expect it. Since it's been six weeks, I'm sure he thinks we wouldn't bother storming the hatch."

He didn't disagree with that. "It's not a bad idea. But you aren't going down there."

"Well, someone has to go unnoticed to get the hatch open. The second the men realize they've been hit, they'll probably override the system so no one can get down there at all. It'll be on lockdown, and the game will be over."

"Then I'll go."

I rolled my eyes. "They'll shoot you the second you walk up to the door."

"They recognize you too."

"Not if I change my hair, makeup, and clothes. I'll go in with a few other women and blend right in."

He shook his head. "I'm not going to say no again."

I would just do it anyway, but since I needed his team to back me up, it was pointless. "I have another idea. But it's more difficult."

"Difficulty isn't an obstacle. But stupidity is."

"It's gotta be possible to either break through that door or override the system."

"Overriding it will be impossible. From inside the hatch, there's got to be some kind of protocol to shut it down. Even if we know the code or force it to open, they must have some fail-safe on their end."

"Then maybe we can drill through it. All we need to do is make a hole big enough to drop a bomb. Problem solved."

Bates watched me for a long time, considering my words carefully. "Like shooting fish in a barrel."

"Yes."

"How big is it down there?"

"Not that big. The drop to the bottom is pretty long, hundreds of feet. We should be able to drop anything without it affecting us. But this all depends on the drilling part."

"I hate Micah as much as you do, but that's pretty cold."

"I agree. But he won't face us like a man."

"Because he knows he'll lose." He rubbed his coarse beard with his palm. "And why fight a war you can't win when you can hide instead?"

It seemed Micah was giving us no choice. We couldn't live knowing he survived, so this war would never truly end. He could either die like a rat or as a man on his own two feet. The choice seemed obvious to me. "I say we give him the option."

Bates raised an eyebrow.

"Call him and tell him what we intend to do. He can decide how he wants to die."

"Or if he knows what we intend to do, he could prevent it."

"How?" I crossed my arms over my chest. "By getting out of the hatch? That's exactly what we want anyway. At least this way, we can instill fear in him...and also have complete control."

Bates lowered his hand and looked at me with new eyes. "You know, you would be the perfect leader for a mob."

"I get that from my father...not that I'm proud of it."

"I think you should be. Cato needs a woman who's tough like him. In fact, I think you're tougher."

I didn't have to be tortured until my knees buckled underneath me, so I couldn't agree with that statement. "So you agree with my idea?"

"I guess so. And I think Micah will give us the answer we want anyway."

"That he'll meet us face-to-face?"

He nodded. "No man wants to die in the bottom of a hole... never to be seen again. We'll talk to Cato."

"What do we do with the rest of Micah's men?"

"That's obvious," he said.

"Kill them?"

"No. They'll become our men. We'll take over their cigar and drug business and keep it as our own. More money in our pockets. That's what conquerors do. They don't invade countries then burn them to the ground. They utilize those resources."

Micah would be replaced by Bates and Cato, and then they would have another business to run. It seemed like their influence stretched on infinitely, never stopping. Every time someone challenged them, it seemed like their power grew, not shrunk. "I guess that makes sense." Micah and Damien had destroyed my family's business and absorbed it. Now it would be Cato's, and by extension, mine. But the last thing I wanted was to be involved in that world again.

It should stay in the past—where it belonged.

————

Martina had fallen asleep beside her father, the keys still clutched in her tiny hand.

Bates sat in the chair at his bedside while I sat at the foot of the bed.

"I think it's a good idea," Bates said. "Like Siena said, it gives us all the power. We're basically manipulating him into doing what we want."

"And if he doesn't cooperate, can we make good on our threat?" Cato asked. "Where we are gonna find a drill that can even accomplish that?"

"The Beck brothers," Bates said. "They've got all that stuff."

Cato nodded in agreement. "That's true."

"Micah knows we know people. He knows we know everyone." Bates rested his ankle on the opposite knee. "I say we make the call and see what he does. It's been six weeks. I'm getting anxious. We've never let an enemy live this long."

"We've never had a rat as an enemy," Cato said. "I want to make the call."

"Are you sure?" Bates asked. "You've been through a lot—"

"That's exactly why I want to do it." Cato glanced down at Martina, probably remembering what it was like when he thought he wouldn't see her again. "This is personal. Very personal."

Bates didn't try to talk him out of it. "Alright. Do you want to wait until you're feeling a little stronger?"

"I'm fine," Cato barked.

"Because when he's out in the open, we'll have to move in—"

"I want to be the one to do it," Cato said. "I can handle it."

I didn't want Cato to exert himself, but I knew reason wouldn't stop him. He'd been beaten nearly to death. Until he had his revenge, he wouldn't stop. Even if Micah wasn't the one to drive that hammer into Cato's body, he was still responsible. I decided to keep my mouth shut this time.

"Alright," Bates said. "When do you want to make the call?"

"Tonight," Cato said. "Then we'll end this—for good."

———

I fed Martina before I put her in her crib. She'd gotten better at sleeping alone, especially after spending all day with her father. I activated her mobile, made sure the baby monitor was on, and then returned to the bedroom.

Cato stood in front of the mirror, fully dressed in black jeans and an olive green t-shirt. It was the first time I'd seen him dressed in nearly two months. He was usually in his boxers or sweatpants because he was too injured to leave the house. He stood upright, his back perfectly straight and his broad shoulders tight. He didn't look like the man who had been returned to me six weeks ago. His muscles had depleted a bit because of his immobility, but he was still the same strong man he used to be.

Instead of telling him to get back into bed, I let him be. I enjoyed taking care of him every day, nursing him back to health so he would be strong once again. He hated being so dependent on another person, thinking he looked weak in my eyes. So I let him have this moment—a moment of triumph. "You look good." I came up behind him and ran my hand down his back.

"Thanks, baby. Clothes are a little loose, but I'll make them fit again soon enough."

"Let's take it easy, alright? No need to rush." I moved in front of him and placed my hands around his wrists, careful not to touch his core in case his ribs still hurt.

The blood lust slowly faded from his eyes as the affection took over. "I can't wait to make love to you."

"Neither can I…"

He grabbed my chin and lifted my head so he could kiss me on the mouth. "I miss you."

"I miss you too." My hands slid up his arms, feeling the muscles that still thrived.

He sucked my bottom lip before he spoke again. "Don't go back on birth control. I want to make another baby with you."

"You're being serious?" I wasn't sure if that was just sexy talk, stuff he blurted out in the moment.

"Dead serious."

"Maybe we should—"

"You want more babies, right?"

"Well, yeah. But I just gave birth to Martina a few months ago…"

"I'm ready whenever you are. If you want to wait, I understand. Think it over." He kissed the corner of my mouth before he turned away and walked out of the room.

I watched him go, wondering if he thought about the obvious thing he never addressed. Martina had been an accident, the product of our insatiable lust and affection. But this baby would be planned, another addition to our family. If that was the case, shouldn't we be married first?

Did he want to marry me?

17

CATO

We congregated in the office, and Siena and Bates wore earpieces so they could hear the conversation with perfect clarity.

I sat near the window and made the call, truly feeling like myself for the first time in six long weeks. I helped Bates with the business, but he did all the heavy lifting without me. All I could do was handle emails in bed and take care of a few phone calls. But I was always in bed, always incapacitated.

But now I was back in the game.

The line kept ringing.

By the fourth ring, Micah answered. But he answered with his silence, probably because he was too afraid to speak first.

I certainly wasn't. "You've been in that rathole for a long time. You must like it down there."

He kept his tone cool like mine, like we weren't two adversaries who wanted to kill one another. "You get used to it. As long as there's booze and pussy, it feels like home. Isn't that all a man really wants?"

"And freedom," I jabbed.

Micah didn't have anything to say to that.

"Bates and I decided how we're going to end this war for good. But then my lovely lady made a very good point. So I'm going to extend some charity to you—man-to-man."

"It took you six weeks to decide?" he asked. "Or it took you six weeks to get out of bed after what Damien did you?"

My blood boiled immediately, and all my old wounds suddenly felt fresh. It would be easy for me to snap and dig into this guy, but the second I lost my temper was the second he won the argument. I couldn't let that happen. I swallowed my rage and kept my tone exactly the same. "It took me six weeks to pick my fantasy—of how I'm going to kill you."

"That hammer must have hurt when it broke each of your ribs."

He tried to change the subject, but I wouldn't let him. "We're prepared to enter your building and drill through the hatch. Once we make a hole large enough in diameter, we'll drop bombs and poison. You don't have a filtration system down there, so the toxins will be trapped with you. If the bombs and the fire don't get you, the poison will slowly kill you. It'll make you bleed from every hole until you go into cardiac arrest." I paused for effect. "The hammer doesn't sound so bad, does it?"

Micah kept his calm even though that threat must have unnerved him. "You'll never be able to drill through the hatch. There's no machinery capable of it in Italy."

"No, not in Italy," I said in agreement. "But the Beck brothers are clients of mine—and they've agreed to let me borrow their biggest drill. He's assured me it'll do the job. The Skull Kings have also agreed to demolish your building so we can get the drill in place. You know there will be no repercussions from law enforcement or the government."

Micah was quiet so long it seemed like he wasn't on the line anymore.

Bates nodded to me, telling me he was still there.

What was Micah supposed to say to that?

I kept my silence so he would squirm. All the information I gave him was valid, so it would be a mistake to call my bluff.

He finally spoke again. "What do you want, Cato? You have a solid plan."

"If it were me, I wouldn't want to die like a fish in a barrel. I'm giving you the opportunity to crawl out of your hole and face me like a man. And die like a man. We both know how this is going to end...but at least you won't die as a coward."

"And you get to look me in the eye as you kill me."

"Exactly." He was responsible for killing Siena's father. Responsible for my kidnapping. Responsible for crimes that needed to be punished. I wanted to see him die at my feet, not wonder if it was the explosion or the poison that got to him first. "And then I want to take your business from underneath your feet—and force your men into my ranks." It would be a transfer of power, a diplomatic conquering. "Your choice, Micah. It's very rare for a man to choose his death. Consider yourself lucky."

He went quiet as he thought it over, considering something most men wouldn't be able to think about. Death was difficult for anyone to accept, but particularly when it was at your doorstep. After what seemed like minutes, he finally spoke, his voice weaker than before. "How will you kill me?"

I knew exactly how. Siena risked herself to save me, and instead of getting my own revenge, I would get revenge for her father. "The same way you killed Stefan Russo." It had been a gruesome death, disgusting enough to make any man vomit in his own mouth. There was no mercy in the murder—and it was completely unnecessary. They hung him from a noose with his hands tied behind his back—and stabbed him to death in the gut. I never told Siena the details because it would haunt her forever.

"I suppose I deserve that..."

"Damn right," I said. "So, what's it gonna be?" I wouldn't want to choke to death on poison, but I wouldn't want to be killed in such a savage way either. But at least the latter let him keep some of his dignity—and made me look like a tyrant.

Micah was quiet again, probably sick as he contemplated his own death. Handing himself over would give him a more brutal death, but at least he would have more respect than letting all of his men die in the hatch with him. "You win, Cato."

I smiled. "I always win, Micah."

———

My body had almost completely recovered, though I still had some pain. But even if I were at my worst, nothing would stop me from finishing this for good. Even if I couldn't walk, I would still have made this happen.

I wore one of my favorite suits even though it was about to be covered in blood. I would have the designer make another for me, and I wanted to look like the tyrant I was as I executed my enemy. We would do it in the middle of the night and leave his body hanging from a pole outside my bank—and the world would know I was victorious.

Siena looked at me in the mirror. "I want to come, Cato."

I tightened my tie around my neck. "Trust me, you don't."

"This is different—"

"It's worse. You couldn't stand watching me shoot those criminals in the head. This will be much more gruesome." I turned around to face her.

She wore a pained expression. "What did he do to my father...?"

I would take it to the grave because it was too disturbing. Now that I loved her, it was even painful for me. I wished I'd been able to save her father so she wouldn't be orphaned. I didn't need anyone, but it was nice having my mother around. If I ever needed someone to talk to, she was always there. Siena had no one—except me. "That's why I don't think you should be there."

"I want revenge—"

"And I will get it for you. Trust me, this is not something you want to see." I cupped both of her cheeks and forced her to look at me. "Baby, please trust me on this. I know you want to see him suffer for what he did to your father and me, but this will not bring you peace. It'll only make you think about how much your father suffered...and that's not what I want."

Siena looked into my eyes, the sadness creeping into her expression.

"Stay here with Martina. I'll be home in less than two hours."

"Alright." She looked like she wanted to argue with me but decided against it. "Be careful."

"I don't need to be careful. Micah already surrendered, and my men picked him up."

"Where are you doing this?"

"Right outside my building."

She raised an eyebrow. "Like, on the sidewalk where the public can see?"

"Yes. And no one will do a damn thing to stop it—because I can't be stopped." I pulled her into my chest and gave her a gentle hug, an embrace that wouldn't aggravate my sore ribs. "I'll see you soon." I pulled away and headed to the door.

"Could you call me when you're on your way back?"

I turned back to her, seeing the genuine concern written all over her face. One night, I was supposed to come home, but I never did. My car didn't make it. I'd been abducted against my will and tortured. "I promise."

"I love you." Her green eyes looked into mine, beaming and bright. Like two stars, they shone brighter than the heavens. Her eyes full of unconditional love and devotion, the loyalty was written all over her face.

Every time she said those words to me now, I said them back. "I love you too, baby."

———

"How are we doing this?" Bates asked from beside me in the car. "Who gets to do the stabbing?"

"Me. All me." I wasn't sharing the execution with anyone else. I was rumored to be a tyrant in this country. I had a reputation to live up to. "It's for Siena's father. Maybe he was a bad man, but he didn't deserve to die that way."

"Shit, no one deserves to die that way." He looked out the window, wearing a black suit with a matching tie. "At least this will be over for good. We'll get their cigar business and wipe their accounts. Easiest money I've ever made."

I didn't care about the money. I just cared about the revenge.

The car pulled up to the curb, and we stepped out.

I had the blade in my pocket, the one I was going to stab my enemy with.

"You're sure you want to wear that?" Bates asked. "I think it's about to get ruined."

"Or it's about to look better."

We moved up the stairs to the front of the building. The metal pole had been set up by my men, and the noose dangled from the apparatus. I pulled the blade out of my pocket and held it at my side.

Bates noticed it. "I'm glad we made up…"

"Yeah, me too. I would hate to waste this knife on you." It was three in the morning, and the streets were quiet. Only a few people passed on the sidewalk, and once they realized something serious was about to happen, they dispersed.

Probably didn't want to be the next victim.

Micah stood off to the side with his wrists bound behind his back. Like a corpse, he was already dead in the eyes, knowing exactly what would happen to him once he was suspended from that rope. He would try not to yell out in pain, but when that knife was deep in his stomach, he wouldn't be able to resist the urge. Like all men before him, he would break. And he would die a horrible death.

I walked up to him with my blade held at my side. "Last words?"

He stared at me with the same look of indifference, like I wasn't worth his time. "Mercy."

"You know I have to do this, Micah."

"But you know where the artery is." He referred to the large one right down his center, the big one that could kill him if it were severed in half. It would only take a few seconds.

"Did you show Stefan Russo mercy?" There was no way to know if his answer was truthful or not, but after being tortured by Damien, I suspected mercy had never been granted. Even after I gave them a truth, Damien still beat me into the ground.

"Damien was the one in charge of that."

That gave me my answer. "So, no." I turned to my men. "Get him up in the noose."

"Let's work out a deal," Micah said. "I'm sure there's something—"

"You tortured and killed my woman's father. Asshole, there's nothing you can say to stop this from happening. Shut up and have some dignity."

My men put the rope around his neck then tightened it. Then they pulled on the level and raised him from the ground, slowly choking him as the rope constricted against his throat.

I gripped the blade in my hand and stared at my enemy, who was a foot higher than me so his stomach was eye level. "I won't pretend I'm not going to enjoy this."

18

SIENA

I couldn't sleep, not until Cato was home. He'd been taken from me once before, and until he walked through that door with those amazing blue eyes, I wouldn't be able to relax. I had the baby monitor on my nightstand and the phone on my chest so I could be attentive to both.

The phone rang.

I answered it right away. "Cato?"

"It's me, baby."

"Are you alright?"

"I'm in the same condition as when I left."

I closed my eyes as the relief swept over me. "When will you be home?"

"About ten minutes. Bates is with me."

"So...is it over?" I didn't ask for the details because Cato said I wouldn't want to know. Maybe he was right. I'd seen enough violence in the last year, and I couldn't handle any more.

"It's over."

"He's dead."

"Yes. My men are taking over his facility as we speak."

I didn't care about that. I just wanted to know that no one was going to hurt us anymore.

"Bates is going to stay with us tonight, but he'll move out in the afternoon."

"He can stay as long as he wants. We've got plenty of room."

"No, he's not welcome with us. He does a lot of kinky shit you don't know about. Trust me, you don't want that depravity in your house."

"Fair enough."

"I'll see you soon. Love you." He said those words to me almost on a daily basis now, and it seemed like he always meant it. It rolled off the tongue so well, like he'd been saying it since the day we met.

"Love you too."

"I'm going to make love to you when I get home." He said the words without shame, not caring if his brother heard every word.

I was so hard up, I didn't care about the breach of privacy. "You better."

———

When Cato came home, he was in a different outfit. He wore jeans and a t-shirt, and the suit he left in was nowhere in sight. He walked into the bedroom a different man than when he left. He was relaxed, relieved, and happy. The corner of his mouth rose in a smile as he looked at me, like he'd been waiting for this moment for a long time.

His shirt came off over his head, and his jeans were next. He stripped down until he was nothing but skin, a hard cock between his legs. He moved into me and slowly pulled his t-shirt over my head, his face close to mine without kissing me. My panties were his next target. He dropped to his knees in front of me and slowly peeled them away while he kissed my inner thighs.

I closed my eyes and dug my fingers into his hair.

He moved his mouth farther up until he kissed my nub, his lips sucking my clit into his mouth. He kissed me with the same passion he would give my mouth, his eyes closed and his hands shaking.

I didn't care that he'd just killed someone. That was the furthest thing from my mind.

He rose to his feet and kissed me on the mouth. "Am I wearing a condom tonight?"

My eyes flashed open. "Why would you wear a condom?"

"You aren't on birth control." His hand slid into my hair, and he breathed close to my mouth. "Unless that means you want to start on baby number two."

I hadn't given it any thought since he'd walked out the door. All I'd cared about was him coming back. "I don't know if that's what I want...but there's no way you're wearing anything." I wanted Cato inside me, skin to skin, and I wanted his come inside me for the rest of the night. If that meant we would have another baby, so be it.

He lifted me into his arms and carried me to the bed. "Good answer."

———

All of Bates's things were packed into the car, and he was ready to leave. "So, I guess this is goodbye." Bates walked up to his brother and clapped him on the shoulder. "We've lived through some pretty crazy shit, huh?"

"Hopefully, this is as crazy as it's going to get," Cato said.

Bates shrugged. "It would be boring if it was. So, are you going to miss me?"

"Not at all." Cato clapped him back. "Giovanni won't miss cleaning up after you and doing your laundry either."

"I don't believe him," Bates said. "It gives him purpose. Well, I'll miss you. It was nice spending that time with you." He didn't look at his brother as he said those tender words.

Cato's eyes softened. "Alright...I'll miss you a little."

Bates grinned. "You'll miss me a lot. I know you will." He came to me next. "I've got your back for the rest of time, Siena. Regardless of what happens between you and my brother...I'll always be there for you." His eyes looked down at Martina in my arms, and he smiled.

"I know you do, Bates. I'll miss you."

His eyes flicked up to mine. "You will?"

"Of course. Water under the bridge, Bates."

He gave me a slight smile before he turned away.

"Wait, aren't you going to say goodbye to your niece?" I placed her in his arms and stepped back so he could hold her.

Bates flinched on the spot, overwhelmed by the gesture. He looked down into Martina's face and wore a subdued look of joy. "Hey, sweetheart. I know we don't spend a lot of one-on-one time together, but I'm your uncle. We have the same eyes."

Cato looked at me, a hint of a smile on his lips.

Bates kissed her on the forehead before he handed her back. "She's beautiful—just like you." He got into his car and drove away.

Cato came to my side and wrapped his arm around my waist. "That was gracious of you."

"He's family...you forgive family."

He brushed his lips against my hairline. "You're a great role model for Martina. She has the best person to look up to."

I looked into my daughter's face and thought of my mother, the woman who had always been my role model. "Thanks...that means a lot to me."

———

I fed Martina as Cato got ready in the morning.

He put on all the pieces of his suit then tied the laces of his shoes.

"Where are you going?" I sat in the armchair while Martina breastfed. My nipples were so raw I could barely feel her sucking lips anymore.

"Work. Where I go every morning."

"Oh..." After everything that had happened, I guess I expected Cato to stop working. All of the horrible things that had happened to us were because of his business. Damien and Micah wanted to overthrow him. That was why we'd experienced this nightmare in the first place.

"Why?" He rose to his full height then smoothed out his navy blue suit.

"Why what?"

"Why would you think I wouldn't go to work? The doctor said I'm fine."

That wasn't why. "I just... I guess I thought you would take more time off."

"All I've done is take time off for the last six weeks. Now that I've recovered, I've got a lot of stuff to do. I've got to manage the new cigar business, and I've been inundated with new clients since I executed Micah."

So, it never stopped. It would never stop. This would be our lives until one of us was killed.

He caught the look in my eyes. "Baby, what's wrong?"

Once the dust had settled, I'd had this daydream that he was going to walk away from the business and we would have the quiet life I always wanted. After almost losing his life and nearly losing me, I'd thought his attitude would change. But it was exactly the same. "Nothing."

19

CATO

Bates fell into the chair facing my desk. He pulled out a cigar as he started to ramble on. "Since the Skull Kings didn't participate, I was able to restore our original agreement—"

"Don't smoke around me." I pointed at his cigar then the ashtray. "Siena doesn't want me to smoke, and I don't want that shit to get in my hair and clothes."

"She's that anal?"

"No. I just don't want to bring it around Martina."

Bates would normally call me a pussy or just do it anyway, but now, he listened to me. He slipped the cigar back into his pocket. "Alright."

"Thank you."

"That means I'm going to have to smoke less...which means I'm going to be healthier...which means I'm going to live longer. And that's entirely your fault." He eyed my liquor cabinet before he grabbed the decanter and a glass. He sat down again and helped himself. "Or maybe my liver will go bad, and I'll die anyway."

"My fingers are crossed."

"As I was saying...the Skull Kings will repay their full debt."

"I'm surprised they agreed to that."

"Well, they didn't have much of a choice. They agreed to provide us a service, and that service was never provided. Henceforth...no deal."

I raised an eyebrow. "Henceforth? Where did you learn that word?"

"Shut the hell up. I read and shit."

"What do you read?" I challenged. "Other than your bank statements."

"I read books, asshole. I read every night before I go to sleep."

"Unless you've paid for a hooker," I countered.

"Which is rare. I don't buy hookers all the time."

"You buy them too much..."

He drank from his glass then rolled his eyes. "What's gonna happen with you and Siena?"

"What do you mean?"

"You're pussy-whipped and she's happy. You're playing house in that big mansion. You told me to make sure she gets everything if you die. I just assumed you were going to marry her at some point."

Siena told me she wanted me for the rest of her life. She wanted to make more babies. She wanted to grow old with me. Marriage was exactly what she wanted. She'd been behaving differently lately, especially when I pressed her on making another baby. I assumed marriage had something to do with it, but she was too proud to ask me about it directly. "When the time is right, I'll ask."

"You'll ask?" He abandoned his drink and gave me his full attention. "Does that mean you have a ring?"

I shrugged. "Maybe I do. Maybe I don't."

"Dude, why won't you just tell me?"

"*Dude*?" I countered. "Is that another word you learned from your books?"

"I don't know why you're being secretive about this. She and I are on great terms now. She even let me hold Martina. Water under the bridge."

That had nothing to do with this. "I'll ask her when I'm ready to ask her. I don't want it to be planned, because life happens while you're making plans. I want it to be spontaneous, in the moment. When that special moment arrives, I'll know it."

"But...do you have a ring?"

"Does it matter?"

"Women like diamond rings."

"Siena doesn't care about stuff like that."

"But it's not very romantic without a ring."

"I never said I didn't have a ring," I countered.

He leaned forward. "So, you do have a ring?"

"I didn't say that either."

He grabbed a piece of paper off my desk, crumpled it, and threw it at me. "I'm your brother, man. Tell me."

"When I ask her, you'll be the first to know. But until then...this is between her and me."

———

I was relieved to be back at the gym. I couldn't run as long as I used to, but I would build back up endurance over time. I couldn't lift the same weight either. My muscles weren't as strong as they used to be, and instead of pushing it too hard, I started easy.

I started over.

I was just grateful to be on my feet again.

After I finished my two-hour workout, I showered and got ready for dinner. "How was your day?" I asked after I shaved in the sink.

"Good. Martina and I went for a walk. There's only a little bit left of summer. Trying to enjoy it."

I patted the aftershave onto my face and then pulled on my clothes.

"How was your day?"

"Good. We made a deal with the Skull Kings. They were supposed to assist us with Micah, but since they didn't, we reverted to our previous deal."

That information seemed boring to her. "Oh."

"How was Martina today?"

"She's good. She's growing so fast, you know. I can see her become more aware of things as she ages. It's like she's beginning to understand we're her parents, this is her home, things like that. She's a sponge, and she's just absorbing everything." She spoke like a typically proud mother.

"She's smart like you."

"More like you. But thank you."

We went downstairs and had dinner. I held Martina in the crook of my arm because I was finally strong enough to do that. I ate with one hand since Siena had been with her all day. Giovanni made us chicken with vegetables, putting us both on low-carb diets. Siena wanted to lose weight after the baby, and I wanted to get back into shape. "I'm glad you and Bates are getting along."

"I couldn't hate someone who loves you so much. Not possible."

Well, I still hated him a bit. Forgiveness wasn't easy for me, unfortunately. Not even when it was my own flesh and blood. You couldn't even see Siena's injury anymore because her hair hid it from view—but I hadn't forgotten.

"You've been doing well in the gym?"

"Yeah. I'm not close to where my strength used to be, but I'll get there."

"Baby steps. No need to rush."

"Yeah, I know." I missed being the most powerful man in the room. Siena still looked at me the same way she used to, like my decrease in size didn't affect her attraction to me. That was the most important thing, that I still turned my woman on.

"I've been working out every day, but I'm not a fan of it."

"I've noticed. Your legs get sexier every time I see you."

She smiled. "Well, I need to work on this gut right now."

I scoffed. "You don't have a gut."

"It's a baby gut. It'll take a while to go away."

"It's not a gut. You're perfect."

"Well, that's nice of you to say, but I still need to hit the gym."

"Unless you become pregnant again." As far as I knew, she hadn't started her birth control again, and we were having lots of sex every night. She seemed hesitant to have another baby right away, but at this rate, we were bound to make one. I'd knocked her up when she was on birth control. I could only imagine how quickly it would happen when she wasn't on it.

"I guess that would give me an excuse to stop the gym," she said with a laugh.

"Especially if you're just going to get sexy again."

"I don't know if being pregnant is sexy…"

"It is to me." I'd never been more attracted to her, watching her waddle around the house and touch her stomach every time the baby kicked. "I hope we have a son this time. If these are the only children we're going to have, I want to have one of each."

"I'd like a son too. I guess we'll see."

20

SIENA

I'd considered telling Cato how I felt.

But it seemed like a moot point to me.

He already knew my feelings.

He knew I didn't want anything to do with this life.

I already had a daughter with him, and considering how much we screwed every night, I was probably having another child soon. Our family had already begun, and I was loyal to him. But I still didn't want this.

I wanted something simple.

Something safe.

I wanted him to give up everything and walk away.

But I knew he never would.

He came home from work that day at his usual time. He walked through the door, gave me a kiss, held Martina, and then stripped off his clothes and got ready for his workout. "You want to have dinner with me tonight?"

"I always have dinner with you."

"But I thought we could do something, just the two of us."

It would be nice not to hold Martina while I tried to eat. She was too young for a high chair, so we had to take turns holding her. The only time we were truly alone was when she was asleep in the next room. And during those times, we didn't talk much. We just made love—over and over.

Not that I was complaining.

"That would be nice. Where do you want to go?"

"I thought we could eat here. We can sit in the backyard and look at the stars."

It was summer, so it didn't get dark until late, but it would be nice to do something different. It would be wonderful to sit by candlelight and look into each other's eyes. Maybe I could forget about the real things that were bothering me. "Oh, that would be lovely."

"Great." He pulled on his t-shirt then kissed me on the lips. "I look forward to it."

————

After I stepped out of the shower, I found the little black dress lying on the bed. Cato wasn't there, but there was a note from him.

Wear this. No panties.

A pair of black heels lay there too.

I smiled as I folded the note. The black dress was short and backless, definitely too slutty to wear out to a restaurant. Maybe that was why he wanted to stay here, so his eyes would be the only ones to look at me.

When I put it on, I realized I couldn't wear panties anyway.

Too sheer for that.

I slipped on the heels, did my hair and makeup, and then made sure Martina was asleep before I headed downstairs. The baby monitor was in my hands because I couldn't go anywhere without it. Even when Martina wasn't with me, she was always in my thoughts. I'd become one of those obsessed mothers who thought only about their children and nothing else.

I wasn't ashamed of that.

"Miss Siena, you look lovely." Giovanni stood in the kitchen, the pots and pans sizzling with whatever he was making for dinner.

"Thanks. Cato picked this out for me."

"He has great taste. And I'm not just talking about the dress."

"Aww...thank you."

Giovanni took the baby monitor out of my hand. "I'll keep an eye on her while you two enjoy yourselves."

"You don't have to do that. I know you're cooking—"

He held up his hand to silence me. "It would be my pleasure. Now, please enjoy yourself."

"Thank you, Giovanni. You're a sweetheart."

"No, Miss Siena. I just like you."

I smiled. "Have you seen Cato? I haven't seen him since he went to the gym."

"He's outside waiting for you."

"Thanks." I walked out the back door and onto the terrace to find him standing in a deep blue suit. He wore a black tie, the watch his brother gave him, and the smile he gave me was brighter than the stars overhead.

"That dress…" He gripped my waist as he leaned down to kiss me. He kissed me softly, like he was doing his best to keep the kiss tame so we wouldn't sneak off into a bush and do what we did best. "I told my personal shopper to get me something short and sexy. She did a good job."

My hand moved down his chest. "She did a good job with you too. How about we skip dinner and just go to bed?" As good as Giovanni's cooking was, it was nothing compared to Cato's fucking. I could never eat again and just live off his lovemaking.

He rubbed his nose against mine. "That's tempting…but the longer we wait, the better it'll be."

"I don't think it could be much better."

His hand moved to my lower back, and he kissed me again. "You know how to make me hard, baby." He guided me down the path with his arm resting just above my ass. "I thought we could eat farther away from the house. You can hear the crickets better. See the stars better."

"I've never been out here in the dark before. It's beautiful."

"I don't take advantage of it as much as I should."

We kept walking until we reached the dining table in the middle of the grass. A wooden platform had been built to hold the table and chairs. A black tablecloth lay over the surface, and white candles were spread out everywhere, illuminating the spot with subtle light.

"Wow...this is beautiful."

He took my hand and guided me up the short steps until we were on the platform. "I'm glad you like it."

"I didn't know Cato Marino could be this romantic."

He pulled out the chair for me so I could sit down before he took the seat across from me. "I didn't either."

"I mean, it took you a year to admit you loved me," I said with a laugh.

"But that doesn't mean I haven't loved you every day since the day I met you." He held my gaze as he spoke, his sincerity bright like the stars above us. "The love started off small, mixed with lust. It grew slowly, persevering despite your lies. And then it grew so big I couldn't ignore it anymore. It was out of my control, a separate living entity. Then one day, it looked me in the face until I had no choice but to accept it."

My eyes softened just like my heart. "Cato..."

"I'm sorry I didn't say it sooner. But I promise I'll say it every day for the rest of my life."

This man had been such an asshole when we met, but now he was the sweetest man in the world. He was a wonderful father to our little girl. He was everything I dreamed of in a man—with one exception. If he loved me this much, then maybe he would give up everything to give me the life I wanted. "I know you will."

A waiter poured us two glasses of champagne and placed an appetizer on our plates.

I laid my napkin across my lap and took a bite of the appetizer, but I felt awkward doing something so normal when Cato had just said something so sweet. His eyes looked even more beautiful in the candlelight. I could see the flames reflected in his eyes. Even in the darkness, they looked more blue, more powerful than ever before. "The stars are incredible." I looked into the sky as I ate, seeing the endless lights across the sky.

Cato kept eating and sipping his champagne. "It's beautiful out here. Quiet. Peaceful. Perfect place to raise a family."

"Yes, it is."

"A bit of a drive to school, but I can drop them off on my way to work."

Anytime he mentioned work, I tensed. How dense could he be? Not once did he wonder if he should walk away from the bank? For his safety as well as his family's?

We finished the appetizer before the main course was brought out. It was a rack of lamb, vegetables, and rice. Just like every night we had dinner together, we ate quietly, looking into each other's eyes as we dined. It was much easier to cut into the meat when I didn't have a baby in one arm. "It's so tender."

"You want to know something interesting about Giovanni?" Cato asked. "He never went to cooking school."

"Really? Seems like it."

"He just has recipes that have been in his family for generations—along with a love of cooking."

"It shows. I enjoy cooking too, but I've always hated doing the dishes."

"Another reason why I need Giovanni. He could ask for a million euro raise, and I would give it to him."

I chuckled. "Me too."

"Speaking of money..." He looked down at his food before he lifted his gaze to look at me again. "I want you to know I changed my trust. If something happened to me, I would leave everything to you."

I was stunned by his statement, considering he'd asked me to forsake all of that just months ago. "You didn't need to do that—"

"I wanted to. Before they took me to surgery, I told Bates to make sure you got everything if I died. You're my family,

Siena. Whether you're my wife or not, you're everything to me. And I want to take care of you. I want to share everything I have, every single euro of my assets. What's mine is yours."

I didn't know what to say. It was a big gesture—and out of character for someone like him. That was his way of telling me he trusted me completely, that all of his walls were finally gone. "That's...very sweet." I appreciated the gesture, even though I actually wanted to leave all of the wealth behind.

The second we finished our meals, the waiter appeared and cleared our plates. Then he placed two brownies with ice cream in front of us.

"Oh my god, that looks delicious," I blurted. "But we're supposed to be dieting."

He shrugged as he picked up a spoon. "It's just one night. Live a little, right?"

I smiled and scooped a large bite into my mouth. "My belly is gonna look so big when we get back to the room."

"No, it's not." He took a few bites until he stopped.

I didn't have the self-control to stop. I ate every single bite and left the spoon on the plate. "Don't judge me."

He smiled. "Never."

The waiter came and took the plates away. We were left with the champagne, the candles, and the stars.

"We should eat out here more often," I said. "It's nice."

"Yeah, it should be a tradition." He leaned back in his chair and stared across his property, his fingers resting along his glass. "I bought this house because I wanted the privacy for my clients. But now I'm glad I bought it to have privacy with you and Martina. We can have our own lives away from everyone else. We can watch the stars without people watching us. I can have a normal life—with the woman I love." His eyes moved to mine across the table. "I've been with a lot of women, but not one of them gave a damn about me. And the only woman who has ever cared about me hated me when she met me. But then she got to know me...and fell hard for me. She loved me despite my flaws. She saw the good instead of the bad. And she proved her loyalty to me...a million times over."

I listened to him pour his heart out to me, observing a version of Cato no one else ever got to see.

"I haven't been whole since my father abandoned me. When I became a man, I didn't think it bothered me. But now I realize it's eaten away at me this whole time, like I've always felt like I had something to prove, like I needed to be someone for another person to actually care. But now that I have you...I realize that's not true. You love me for me, not my money or my power. And now I feel whole...for the first time in my life."

I smiled and felt my eyes water at the same time. It was easy to forgive him for the wrongs he committed when he said things like that. He was still a boy with a heart of gold underneath all that man. He was a sweetheart. I saw it every time he interacted with Martina.

"I love you, baby. With all my heart." He looked at me over the candles. "You have all of me—wrapped around your finger."

"I love you too, Cato." He was the only man I'd ever loved. He was the only man I ever wanted to love.

He reached into his pocket then pulled out a small box, a box that could fit a ring.

That's when I stopped breathing.

He opened the box and placed it in front of me, revealing a small diamond ring. A white-gold band with a simple diamond in the middle, it was sleek, simple, and humble. It fit my personality exactly.

I watched it reflect the lights of the candles, the clarity obvious flawless. It might be small, but it was the highest quality diamond on earth.

He watched my reaction as he left the box in front of me, his blue eyes watching mine stare at the ring in shock.

"Marry me." It wasn't a question. It was a command. I would be his wife no matter what.

I stared at the ring again, feeling the happiness burst inside my chest. My natural impulse was to say yes. I wanted to spend the rest of my life with this man, to grow our family, and grow old together until we were buried together in the same cemetery where my parents rested.

But there was something I needed first.

Cato's eyes darkened in pain when he didn't get the reaction he wanted.

"I'm not saying no..." I brought the ring closer to me, admiring its simple beauty. But I didn't take it out of the box and put it on my hand.

"Siena." His pain became more noticeable—like I was breaking his heart. "I don't understand. You love me. I love you. We have a daughter. What...what more do you want from me?"

"You know what I want, Cato." I closed the box so the beautiful ring wouldn't tempt me anymore.

"I really don't."

I knew this man loved me, so he would probably give me what I wanted. It was a sacrifice he should make whether I was in the picture or not. "I can't live like this..."

"Like what? In a mansion? With a rich husband? Under the stars? What does that mean?"

"Cato, you almost died. Let's not forget what happened."

His eyes narrowed. "I'm not following, Siena. I'm really not."

"In your line of work, we'll never be safe. There will be periods of peace before there are periods of war. It'll happen in a cyclical pattern, but one of us might die during a war period. My father didn't take me seriously, and he lost my mother. Then he lost his own life. You and I got lucky. Really lucky. We won't get lucky again."

His eyes softened as he listened to me. "What are you suggesting?"

"I want you to quit."

"Quit?" he asked. "There's nothing to quit. I own the company."

"Then sell it. Give it to Bates. Step aside...and let's have the simple life I want."

He digested everything I said, his eyes still hard. It took him a long time to come up with a response. He glanced at the ring and looked at me again. "Are you giving me an ultimatum?"

"I...guess so."

He sat back against the chair, sighing.

"Walk away, Cato. Take your money and walk away."

"And do what?" he countered. "I will have no purpose."

"What about Martina and me? Isn't that your purpose? The only purpose that really matters?"

"Of course. But I need more than that. I'm an ambitious man. If I'm home all day, I'll get angry. Then I'll get resentful."

"Then open a business—a clean business. The Barsettis were criminals until they walked away and started making wine. That could be you."

"How did you know that?" he countered.

"My father used to be friends with Crow."

"Well, I'm not Crow Barsetti. I'm much richer than Crow Barsetti."

"The amount of wealth doesn't matter," I argued. "You just told me you feel whole for the first time in your life. That's because of us—not the money in your bank account. Just walk away."

He shook his head slightly. "That's my life's work."

"I know. You should be proud of everything you've accomplished. But you're also a crime lord, and one day, someone is going to come after us. I can't let that happen to our babies..." My eyes watered in pain. "I have to protect them. I have to protect myself—"

"*I* will protect you." He slammed his fist down.

"How can you do that when you can't protect yourself?" I asked quietly.

His eyes turned ice-cold.

"I was the one who saved you, Cato."

"I never asked you to do that. I never wanted you to do that."

"But we're a team. I don't regret it. But all of that happened because of your business. You need to walk away—to keep us all safe. That's what I want."

"Siena—"

"It's not just what I want. It's what I need." I wiped my tears away. "I don't want to say this. It kills me inside. But if you want me to marry you...you have to do this."

His breathing picked up, and his eyes clouded with a thin film of moisture. They turned glossy in the light from the candles.

"You know I love you. You know I want to say yes. I would never ask you to give up anything...but you have to give this up. I won't change my mind. So, please...do this for me."

He rubbed his hand across his mouth and sighed.

"Cato."

Now he wouldn't look at me.

"Cato."

"You're asking me to walk away from...everything I've built."

"I know."

"You're asking me to give up who I am."

"You're more than that. You are more than what you do."

"You need to meet me halfway here, Siena. How can you ask this of me when my business paid for all this shit?" He extended his hands as he looked around. "Those expensive sheets you sleep on every night. The bathroom that's as big as a house. The gourmet meals you eat every night—"

"I. Don't. Care. About. That." I hit my fist against the table with every word. "We could move back into my old place, and I would be just fine. I've never wanted you for the luxuries you provide. If I had it my way, I would want you to donate all your money, and we would just live off what we needed."

With a clenched jaw, he looked at me like that had just made him angry.

"I'm sorry..."

His nostrils flared as he sighed.

"Are you really going to pick your business over us?" I asked incredulously. "You really want to lose me because of money?"

"It's not about the money. I've told you that."

"Whatever. Is it really more important than us?"

"It's not more important. I just don't see why I can't have both—"

"Because we both could have died! It will happen again, Cato. Maybe it won't happen for a few years, but it will happen. Are you so arrogant to assume you're that untouchable? Those men hit your car and kidnapped you without a fuss."

He breathed through his anger.

"I want to cave...I do. But this really bothers me, Cato. Give up the business and be with us...or keep the business and we go our separate ways." I couldn't believe those words flew out of my mouth. I couldn't believe I even suggested us breaking up.

"You're gonna take my daughter away?" he asked incredulously.

"No. Never. But...we'll live somewhere else."

He shook his head. "This is a fucking nightmare. I planned all of this so you could be my fucking wife, and you drop this on me?" He rose to his feet, furious. "You couldn't have mentioned this yesterday? Or the day before?"

"I meant to, but—"

"Shut up."

Now I rose to my feet, my ferocity matching his. "You never trusted me because you thought I wanted your money. I've proved to you it means nothing to me. You're the one who's obsessed with your money, who loves it more than me. You're really going to walk away from the best thing that ever happened to you over money." I gripped my skull. "Do you realize how pathetic that makes you?"

"It's not about money," he hissed. "That company gives me purpose. It makes me feel like a man. It turned me into a fucking man. That job got my mom out of the cannery and gave me enough money to rent my first apartment. That company is full of my blood, sweat, and tears. It's not about money."

Tears ran down my cheeks. "You're still choosing it over us."

"Only because you're making me."

When I heard his final decision, I started to sob. "You said you loved me more than anything."

"And I do." He slammed his hand into his chest. "I would die for you."

"You would die, but you won't walk away from your company?"

"You know what I mean."

"No," I snapped. "I *don't* know what you mean." I tried to wipe my tears away, but it was no use. They just kept coming. "I can't believe you're doing this. You said you would always protect me, but you're continuing to put us in harm's way. Why don't you see that?"

"I would never let anything happen to you—"

"Goodbye, Cato." I walked past him and headed down the stairs and to the pathway. This conversation kept going in circles, and it would never stop. I asked him for the one thing that mattered, and he refused to give it to me.

He would rather lose me over his company.

Lose his family over his company.

I couldn't reason with greed. I couldn't reason with money. I couldn't reason with wealth.

I could only reason with love.

But he couldn't.

————

It was too late in the evening to flee the estate, so I went into the bedroom and gathered all the things I would need tomorrow. I stuffed all my clothes and accessories inside plastic bags then carried them into my old bedroom down the hall. I left his bedroom exactly as I found it—with no trace of me.

I went into Martina's bedroom with the intention of taking her with me, but when I saw how angelic she looked, I chose to stand there and stare at her. The most beautiful thing I'd ever made was right in front of me—and she was half Cato. I made sure I didn't cry as I stood there so I wouldn't disturb her, but the emotion was wreaking havoc in my chest.

This was really over.

I could have kept my mouth shut and not cornered Cato, but I wouldn't have been happy. I would always be scared, waiting for the next blow to strike us. Anytime my children were at school or staying at a friend's house, I would be a mess until they returned. My life would be centered around worrying, worrying about the moment when someone would try to kill all of us.

If it were just me, maybe it was a risk I could take.

But not with Martina.

I couldn't let anything bad ever happen to her.

What kind of mother would I be?

I watched her for a few moments before I left the room and went to my old bedroom, to the place where I used to live when I meant nothing to Cato. It was more luxurious than a five-star hotel, but I would prefer to sleep with Cato in a sleeping bag than be in here alone.

I got into bed without taking off my dress and cried.

Because the man I loved didn't love me enough.

I'd risked my body and my dignity when I gave myself to Damien. That outcome could have been completely different. I might have been his prisoner a long time, and I would have been raped and tortured until someone saved me. I risked that for Cato—but he couldn't do this for me.

When dawn arrived, I carried everything downstairs to the driveway. It was still cool after the long night, and I was exhausted from not sleeping at all. I'd just lain there, crying on and off throughout the night.

"Miss Siena, what are you doing?" Giovanni asked me in the entryway. He glanced at my hand, expecting to see the diamond ring Cato offered me.

"Martina and I are leaving. I need someone to drive us to my old place."

"Of course…" His hands came together, and he slightly fidgeted in place. "I…I'm so sorry."

"I am too. But it didn't work out." I moved past him.

Giovanni stepped in front of me again. "I don't mean to overstep my boundary, but I assure you that Mr. Marino loves you with all his heart. Instead of fleeing, perhaps you should talk to him."

"We've done enough talking, Giovanni. I told him I wouldn't feel safe until he stepped away from his line of work…and he refused. After everything that's happened, I can't put our daughter through that. So…my answer was no."

He gave a slight nod, his eyes filled with sadness. "He'll come around."

"I don't think he will." I stepped around him once more. "Cato is a stubborn man, but this isn't stubbornness." I moved up the stairs again and returned to my room. I gathered my final things before I dropped them off on the doorstep. Then I retrieved Martina along with her bag of essentials.

Cato's door was still closed.

I was sure his men had informed him I was preparing to leave, but he didn't try to argue with me. He didn't see me off. He kept the door shut, giving me a cold goodbye. He didn't even come out to kiss Martina.

I stared at the door for another minute before I walked away, choking back tears at his coldness. We'd been so deeply in love days ago, and now that love had disappeared. It was like it never happened in the first place.

I walked outside and found the car waiting for me.

Distraught, Giovanni stood there with redness in his eyes. "I'm sorry to see you go, Miss Siena. I didn't expect this, not after everything we've been through."

"Me too." I hugged him and kissed him on the cheek. "Goodbye, my friend."

"He'll come around, Miss Siena. That man loves you too much not to."

"I hope you're right." I got into the car and put Martina in the car seat. Then the car slowly started to pull away, circling the roundabout and the fountain. The gravel crunched under the tires as we left the property. I looked up at the three-story estate and wondered if Cato was watching me leave his life forever. Or if he was still in his bedroom, shutting me out because I'd hurt him so much.

Whatever hurt he thought he felt, I felt it a million times more.

He said loyalty was the most important thing to him. But when it came down to it, he wasn't loyal to me. I'd sacrificed myself to save him, but he wouldn't make sacrifices for me. At the end of the day, he made the same mistakes as my father. His arrogance blinded him to the truth, made him think he was invincible. My mother died because of my father's stupidity. But I wouldn't be let anything happen to me because of Cato's stupidity. Cato didn't learn from other people's mistakes.

But I sure did.

———

The air was stuffy and stale, but it was exactly the way I remembered it. I would have to get a new battery in my car because it was definitely dead by now. There were dishes still in the sink, and a pile of folded laundry sat on the couch.

It'd been so long that I couldn't remember the last time I was here.

"This is our new home, Martina." I held her in my arms as we stepped inside the living room, her body resting on my shoulder.

Instantly, she started to cry.

She knew this wasn't her home.

She knew her father wasn't here.

She knew everything was different.

Someone knocked on the door, which made Martina cry harder.

I opened the door and came face-to-face with one of Cato's security men. "Yes?"

"Mr. Marino asked us to bring some things and set them up." In his hands, he had a box with a picture of a crib on it. The other men behind him all carried something, toys, diapers, and everything else I needed to take care of Martina long term.

"Oh...thank you. Set it up in the empty bedroom."

Setting up baby stuff probably wasn't in their job description, but they didn't complain as they went upstairs and got to work.

Martina wouldn't stop crying.

———

Martina was constantly fussy.

She cried more than she ever had before. I checked her diaper, tried to feed her, and rocked her back and forth. Nothing worked. I abandoned the crib and had her sleep with me, but she didn't like that either.

I knew exactly why she was crying.

Because she missed her father.

I missed him too.

Anytime I looked outside, I saw army men around the perimeter of my property. Cato must have asked them to guard me, to make sure no one bothered the two of us. It was strange to look outside in the middle of the day and see the black cars everywhere, but I knew there was no other option.

After four days of silence, Cato called me.

I stared at the screen for a long time, my heart falling into my stomach. This moment was inevitable so I shouldn't be surprised, but I still felt my nerves fire off in fear. Martina was still crying, so I put her in her crib and went downstairs—that way I could actually hear what he had to say. I answered. "Hi..." I missed the sound of his voice. I missed his strong body in my bed. I missed the quiet noises he made when he slept.

He was just as pissed off as the night I rejected his proposal. "I want to see my daughter. I'm not asking for permission."

I felt stupid for thinking he would be sweet and apologetic. I hoped he would say he missed me so much that he would give me whatever I wanted. But instead, he was as livid as before. "You never have to ask for permission, Cato."

He paused before he answered. "I'm outside."

"I'll open the door." I hung up and opened the door.

He was in his suit, like he just got off work. In navy blue with a gray tie, he looked exactly as sexy as I remembered. Tall, muscular, and beautiful, he was absolutely gorgeous. There was a slight hint of affection in his eyes when he looked at me, but it was quickly masked by his rage. Martina cried from upstairs, so he let himself inside and went to retrieve her.

I shut the front door then listened to Martina stop crying.

Instantly.

I walked upstairs and watched them together.

Cato held her in his arms as he looked down into her face, his eyes lighting up with love. "Hey, sweetheart." He kissed her forehead as he gently rocked her from side to side. "Missed you."

I leaned against the doorframe. "She's been crying nonstop since we left. And now I know why...she misses you."

He lifted his gaze to look at me, his affection slowly disappearing. "I want her half the week. You get her the other half."

I couldn't believe we were having this painful conversation, like a divorced couple arguing over custody. "What about when you're at work all day?"

"I'll get a nanny."

I didn't want a stranger watching my child. "I'm home during the day. How about I watch her during the day, and then you pick her up on your way home. Then we can trade weekends." Was I stupid for thinking Cato would come to his senses and change his mind? Maybe I underestimated how much he loved his company. Maybe I never had a chance of being more important. I'd handed myself over to a psychopath, but that didn't seem to count for anything.

"You'll need to go back to work eventually."

"I'll work nights until she starts school."

Cato's eyes flashed with hostility, as if he didn't like that.

"You know what's ironic?" I crossed my arms over my chest, knowing my words would piss him off. "You care so much about loyalty...wanted to kill me because I wasn't loyal to you. But when it mattered most, you weren't loyal to me."

He stopped bouncing her from left to right.

"Damien came to my house and threatened to rape me and torture me if I didn't cooperate. That happened because my father didn't get out of the business when he should have, even when my mother was kidnapped, raped, and tortured. They came after his daughter next...me. I did my best to save him, but he was dead long before I proved myself. Even when I distanced myself from my family, I was still a target by association. Then I handed myself over to Damien to save your life...the last thing I wanted to do. But despite all that history, you still don't see what I'm saying. I was attacked for being my father's daughter. You really think Martina won't be attacked for being your daughter someday?"

Cato held my stare, his look neither angry or apologetic. It was impossible to tell if my words resonated with him because he showed no reaction. After minutes of silence, he grabbed her favorite blanket and wrapped it around her before he took her upstairs.

I didn't know what was about to happen.

Cato suddenly walked past me, down the stairs, and out of the house.

The second he shut the door behind him, Martina started to cry.

21

CATO

My life turned into a dull routine.

I worked out, went to work, and then came home. I moped around the house, drowning my sorrow in booze, and then I passed out and went to sleep. When I woke up the next morning, I did it all over again.

I missed seeing Martina every day when I came home from work. Even though I got to work out in the morning again, I missed waking up early to take care of her before heading off for the day. It was the only part of the day when it was just the two of us.

I missed Siena too.

But I was too pissed at her to admit that to myself.

Her ring sat in my nightstand drawer even though I was seriously tempted to throw it away. When I'd originally bought her ring, I almost got one with an enormous rock in the center, along with more diamonds in the band. But then I realized that didn't match Siena's personality at all. She didn't want to be covered in jewels.

So I went with something simpler.

Like her.

I knew she loved it, even if she never told me.

But then she dropped that ridiculous request on me, like it was something I could honor. She said she loved me for me, and that was supposed to include all the elements of my life, including my job.

I understood her request. I would be stupid to say it wasn't a legitimate concern. But I was pissed she had that kind of power over me, that she could say no to me and make her own demands. I told her that was my biggest fear, having someone rule me so easily.

It left a bad taste in my mouth.

Maybe I was just being stubborn or arrogant, but I refused to change my mind.

No matter how much I loved her.

———

Bates sat across from me as he flipped through the pages. "Then we include a bunch of bullshit about the terms and blah, blah..." He flipped more pages. "They sign here and here, and then we're millions of dollars richer. Piece of cake." He clapped his hands together. "Ooh...cake sounds pretty good."

I stared at him but didn't listen to a word he said. My job had given me no pleasure that week. After executing Micah, everything seemed boring. It was just more money and more bullshit. With Siena gone, I was starting to feel the way I did before we met—unfulfilled.

Bates kept rambling on about cake. "I can't even remember the last time I had cake. I only eat carbs on holidays, and there's usually no cake at those sorts of things. Maybe I'll have a cheat day. Maybe I'll bring over one of my ladies and rub cake all over her."

I couldn't care less about his sex life.

When Bates noticed I was barely listening, he tossed the papers on the desk. "Where are you?"

"Sitting across from you."

He tapped his fingers against his skull. "No. Where are you?"

"Just got a lot on my mind."

"You've been weird all week. What's the deal?"

"I'm not weird," I countered. "You talk a million miles an hour. I have less to say."

"No. I know there's something bothering you." He pointed at me, scolding me. "I didn't say anything for the first few days because I thought it would pass, but clearly, it's not going to. It's because you miss me at the house, huh?"

I rolled my eyes. "Not even a little bit."

"Then what is it? Everything okay with Siena?"

Just hearing her name caused me pain. I slept in that enormous bed alone without my lady beside me. I went to bed hard and horny because I couldn't make love to her. I couldn't go out and pick up pussy somewhere else because Siena was the only pussy I wanted. "It didn't work out."

"What didn't work out?" he asked, his eyebrow raised.

"Us."

Bates still took several seconds to understand what I was saying. "What the hell happened? You were in love and shit. What did you do?"

"What makes you think I did anything?"

His eyes narrowed, full of accusation.

I looked away, hating the truth in his gaze.

"Talk to me, Cato."

"I'm good." I grabbed the papers and tossed them back. "Just get these signed, and let's move forward."

Bates held the papers but stared at me incredulously. "You seriously aren't going to tell me?"

"No." Just admitting the truth to myself was difficult. I thought I had everything, and then an instant later, I lost it at all. I'd never felt so alone. Not hearing my daughter's cries down the hallway broke my heart. Not listening to Siena sing in the shower broke my heart too. "Drop it, Bates."

A shadow passed over his gaze, a storm of pain and hurt. He'd gotten upset with me many times in our lives, but he'd never looked quite like this—like he was actually offended. He gathered the papers then left my office without another word.

22

SIENA

I was feeding Martina a bottle that night when the doorbell rang.

It was almost eight in the evening, so I assumed it was Cato stopping by for a visit. I was in my pajamas with my hair in a bun, but I didn't have a chance to fix myself up in any way. My hand held the bottle to her mouth as I walked to the door and opened it.

But it wasn't Cato.

It was Bates.

With a serious expression and a hint of sadness in his eyes, he didn't look like himself. He stepped inside and shut the door behind himself.

Bates was the last person I expected to show up on my doorstep. "Everything alright?"

"No. You're living here, while my brother lives alone. Nothing is alright." He looked down at Martina but didn't give her the look of affection he usually did. "Cato has been in a mood all week, but I thought it would pass. When I confronted him about it today, he told me you guys split up—but he didn't tell me why." He looked at the TV, which showed the nightly news. He grabbed the remote and turned off the screen, so we were surrounded by silence. "So, why?"

"He's gonna be pissed when he finds out you're here."

"I don't give a shit. He's always pissed at me." He sat on the couch and tapped the cushion beside him. "So, talk to me."

I carried Martina then sat beside him. She continued to suck on her bottle, her eyes open and staring at her uncle. I'd started pumping so she wouldn't make my nipples even more sensitive. "He didn't tell you anything?"

He shook his head. "And I have a feeling he did something stupid. He always does something stupid. He says I'm the dumb one, but I don't fuck up relationships as much as he does."

"So...did he tell you he proposed to me?"

When his eyes snapped wide open, that was my answer. "No. When?"

"A week ago."

"And I'm guessing you said no...? Although, I have no idea why you would. My brother is the best guy I know. He's rough around the edges sometimes and he's made mistakes, but he loves you, Siena. Like, really loves you."

"I know he loves me. But he doesn't love me enough."

"What are you talking about?" he whispered. "What did you say when he asked you to marry him?"

"I didn't say no...but I didn't say yes. I told him he had to give up his business if he wanted to marry me. As long as he continues to be part of that company, we'll always be in danger. And I can't do that to Martina...or any other children we have. After everything that's happened with my family, I thought he would understand that. After everything we just went through, I thought he would understand that. But he said no..."

Bates stared into my eyes in genuine bewilderment, like he couldn't believe the story I'd just shared with him. His hands moved into his lap, and he turned his gaze forward, contemplating everything I'd said. "So, he picked the company over you?"

I nodded. "Said he wouldn't change his mind. But I won't change my mind either."

He sighed quietly, shaking his head. "That doesn't make any sense."

"Well, that's what happened…"

"I've seen Cato every day, and he's miserable. He's not even focused in the office. His mind is always somewhere else. And before he met you, he told me he felt bored…that it's the same shit every day. I know his job doesn't give him a lot of fulfillment anymore. And the only time I ever see him happy is when he's with you. So, this isn't making any sense."

"I don't understand it either."

Bates rubbed his palm along his jaw, sighing quietly. "He'll come around. I know he will. There's something more complicated going on with him. I'll talk to him."

"I know he must have been hurt by my reaction." He'd poured his heart out to me under the stars, saying the sweetest things I didn't think he was capable of. He'd turned into the tenderest and more caring man I'd ever known. And then he asked me to marry him…only to be rejected. "Maybe that wounded his pride. He does have an ego. But I don't want to build a life with him under these circumstances. I have to keep my family safe, and as long as he continues to be involved with this business, we'll always be targets. We have to learn from the past..."

"I understand, Siena. Really, I do." He patted my thigh. "I'll talk to him."

"I'm not sure how well that's going to go."

"It won't go well at all," he said with a chuckle. "But I have to try. You're the best thing that's ever happened to him. I'm not going to let him throw you away."

I smiled at him. "That's sweet of you..."

"I don't know what's going through my brother's mind, but he's obviously in a bad place."

"Maybe he feels too guilty leaving you to handle the company on your own."

He shook his head. "Ideally, I'd like him there. But I'd understand if he wanted to step down. I can handle it on my own. Besides, I want my brother to be happy. How could I be mad at him for being happy?"

I rubbed his arm and felt my affection for him grow. "Whether Cato and I end up together or not, I love you, Bates. I love you like a brother." I rested my head against his shoulder and linked my arm through his.

He stayed still as he felt me lean against him. It seemed like he had nothing to say, and the silence lingered between us. Then he rested his head against mine and sighed. "I love you too, Siena."

23

CATO

The second Bates arrived at her doorstep, I knew he was there.

And it was only a matter of time before he ended up on my doorstep too.

Nosy fucking asshole.

Two hours after he arrived at Siena's house, he came to my front door and stepped into the entryway. My men told me when he approached the gate at the end of the driveway, so I walked downstairs in my sweatpants and waited for him to walk inside.

He opened the door himself and crossed the threshold, because he was the only person in the world who had the right. He came face-to-face with me, and when he saw the pissed expression I wore, he knew I knew everything. "You should have told me yourself."

"I didn't expect you to go behind my back."

"I didn't go behind your back. She has my niece." He was still in his suit because he went straight to Siena's at the end of the workday. "She's still family. And I have to make sure you don't fuck up the greatest thing that ever happened to you."

"Well, too late," I said bitterly.

"Too late?" he asked. "It's definitely not too late."

I crossed my arms over my chest and stared my brother down in the entryway. I was livid with him for talking to Siena, but since I didn't confide in him myself, I couldn't be too angry with him.

"She's miserable without you."

And I was miserable without her.

"Why are you doing this? Just give her what she wants. It's not like her request is unfounded. Her family was wiped out because of the shit we do on a daily basis. She wants her life to be different." He slid his hands into his pockets and kept several feet in between us. "If you're worried about me, don't be. I'll be fine, Cato. And you even told me how bored you are. We did that deal with the Chinese, made millions, and you looked out the window and said you were bored. You're definitely not bored with Siena. So giving up your stake in the company shouldn't be difficult."

I didn't expect anyone to understand how I felt. No matter how many times I explained it, it seemed like all I cared about was money. "My entire adult life has been about that company. It aged me, hardened me. It turned me from a boy into a man. It was the first time I stood on my own two feet and proved I didn't need anyone else. I didn't need Mother to take care of me—I took care of her. I proved to our father that I turned out fine without him to raise me. I proved to the world, to my friends as well as my enemies, that I was the most powerful man in this country."

Bates listened but looked slightly confused, as if he didn't understand why I was saying all of this.

"That's the man Siena met. The powerful, dominating, wealthy man who could make anything happen. Without that company...I'm just a man. I'm not special. I'm not different. Siena is a strong woman who needs a strong man. What am I without that company?"

"Cato...you're the exact same man you were before. You don't need it as a crutch anymore. Maybe it was your identity in the beginning, but it's not anymore. She loves you for you, the man in sweatpants, not the man in the suit. Just walk away from it."

I bowed my head as I considered it. "She gave me an ultimatum. I asked her to marry me, and she gave me a fucking ultimatum."

"Because she knows what kind of life she wants. You have to agree on that before you spend your lives together."

"I don't appreciate being told what to do," I snapped. "I don't appreciate her calling the shots and deciding what happens with us. I'm the one in control. I'm the provider. I'm the man."

He shook his head slightly. "That might work with other women, but it won't work with Siena—and that's why you love her. You're sharing the power with her. That's what a marriage is. You're going to have to accept that if you want to keep her. She's not trying to emasculate you. She's just trying to protect her kids. You need to drop your ego and realize you're going to have to compromise every single day for the rest of your life."

I never compromised. I always got what I wanted. I was always the one in charge—because that guaranteed that everything would go my way. Now this woman had made me fall in love with her, and she'd asked me to turn my back on my entire way of life. She asked me to give up my company and turn to a quiet existence. Maybe it was just a job to her, but it was my entire identity. I was the richest and more fearsome man in Italy. Now I would just be... a man.

"All that matters is this—you love her. You can't live without her. The three of you are a family. So just give her what she wants. You can either cave and be happy...or be stubborn and be miserable for the rest of your life."

24

SIENA

Martina hadn't calmed down since we started living alone.

She missed her father all the time.

It was incredibly sweet, but also heartbreaking.

I missed our old home. I missed Cato. I missed the life we used to have...as a family.

But Cato continued to refuse me.

After breakfast that morning, I hurried upstairs when I heard Martina crying. I barely made it to her crib before I had to take a detour and rush to the bathroom. I suddenly felt sick to my stomach, and just as I reached the toilet, I threw up.

My breakfast came up, and once the food was out of my stomach, I felt better.

Must have been the eggs.

When I remembered the last time I was sick like this, I leaned against the wall and nearly lost my breath. I'd been sick every morning until the realization hit me—that I was pregnant. Without even taking a pregnancy test, I knew the truth. "Why does Cato always get me pregnant...?" For a brief moment, I was happy, imagining having a son in his likeness. But then I remembered the situation we were in... and we weren't even together.

Martina saved my life, and maybe our second baby would save our relationship. Even when we tried to get away from away each other, our daughter bound us together. Now it was happening again.

I stayed in the bathroom and listened to my daughter cry in the other room. I knew she was just being fussy, so I stayed on the ground and tuned her out. I knew Cato would be happy when I told him the news, and maybe he would be happy enough to give me what I wanted.

Or maybe it would make no difference at all.

My phone rang in my back pocket, so I pulled it out and checked the screen.

It was a number I didn't recognize.

I answered it. "This is Siena."

"Hey, Siena." His deep voice was innately powerful, holding authority without having to earn it. "It's Crow Barsetti."

I hadn't spoken to him in a year. During our last conversation, I was still trying to figure out how to capture Cato. He was the one who got me the job as Cato's art collector. "Hey...how are you? It's been a while."

"I'm good," he answered. "We just celebrated Crow Jr.'s second birthday."

"Aww...that's nice." Now that I had my own daughter, I understood how wonderful it was to have children.

"How are you?" he asked. "I've noticed that you and Cato have...settled down."

"We did...but we recently broke up."

"Really?" he asked. "Even though you have a daughter?"

"It's a long story..."

"I have the time if you do."

"Well..." I told him Cato wouldn't give up his life in the criminal underworld so I was left on my own. I also mentioned my father. "I was able to bury my father with my mother. Cato made that happen...so I'm eternally grateful."

"That is nice. I never had the opportunity to bury my parents, only my sister."

"I'm sorry."

"It's okay," he said. "It was a long time ago. About Cato...I understand it's hard for a man to walk away from something he built with his own hands. It defines him as a man, gives him power. It's addictive...to walk into a room and know you're the most powerful man there. There's no man in the world who doesn't get off on that feeling. To give all that up...for the unknown...would be hard for anyone."

"So, I'm being unrealistic?"

"Not at all," he said. "You're right about everything. It's not about if, but when. Someone will try to hurt Cato, and the best way to do that is to hurt you and your kids. Preferably, your kids. If he wants to protect his family, hanging up the towel is his only option."

"But he won't do it."

"He may just need some time. Is he a good father?"

I smiled when I pictured him with Martina. "The best."

"Then he'll come around. He just wants to come to this decision on his own—his own terms. Makes it feel like less of a sacrifice."

"It's been almost two weeks, and he hasn't done that already..." It'd been the longest two weeks of my life. I kept waiting for him to walk through the door so he could take us back home, but he never did. I expected phone calls in the middle of the night, telling me he loved me and missed me. But that didn't happen either.

Crow was quiet.

"I know this is probably a lot to ask...but would you mind talking to him?"

Crow didn't say anything.

"You don't have to if you don't want to. But maybe hearing this story from another powerful man will make him see reason."

"He might just shoot me."

"Not if I'm there. He would never hurt you if I asked him not to."

He still didn't give me an answer.

"I know you said you didn't want to be involved in anything—"

"I'll do it. I couldn't help you before, but I can help with you this. It's just a conversation, right?"

I stared at the bathroom wall while a feeling of hope exploded inside my chest. "Thank you...so much."

25

CATO

Bates stepped inside my open door. "Talk to her yet?"

I kept my eyes on my laptop. "You already know the answer."

"Then let me rephrase it. *When* are you going to talk to her?"

"Bates." I said his name in a warning tone. "Just butt out."

"I'm your brother. It's my responsibility to make sure you don't do anything stupid. And that goes both ways."

"You're being stupid right now."

He stepped back into the hall and gestured to someone. "There are a few people here to see you."

"Who?"

A tall man with dark brown hair stepped inside. With hazel eyes, tanned skin, and in black jeans and a matching shirt, he looked familiar right away. He was a man in his late fifties, but he moved like he was in his early twenties. He approached my desk, holding my gaze like he wasn't afraid of me—but he wasn't hostile either.

Siena walked in behind him, beautiful in a deep blue sundress and a yellow cardigan. Martina wasn't with her. She looked slightly guilty for ambushing me, but she didn't apologize for it.

I was angry with her, but it was hard not to love her when she looked so beautiful. Her hair was curled the way I liked, and she wore the bracelet I gave to her for Christmas. She stood beside the man I didn't know. "Cato, this is Crow Barsetti...a friend of mine."

Crow didn't reach out his hand to shake my hand. Most men who stepped into this office immediately kissed my ass, but he didn't bother with the practice. He gave a slight nod of acknowledgment.

I finally took my eyes off Siena to really look at Crow. "We've met before."

"But it's been almost ten years." He lowered himself into the armchair and crossed his legs. "I hear you're a fan of my wine."

"I am." I looked at Siena again, not understanding the purpose of this meeting.

She sat beside him. "You and Crow have a lot in common. I thought he could tell you his life story...and maybe it would resonate with you."

I remembered she'd mentioned him recently, that he gave up his life in crime for a simple one in the countryside. He did it to protect his family, and now she wanted him to talk me into doing the same thing. The gesture annoyed me. "You think I give a damn what this man has to say? That's his life—not mine."

"Could you just listen?" she asked quietly. "It's the least you could since I saved your life."

She threw that in my face every chance she got. "Fine. But I want to talk to him alone."

Siena stiffened at the request. "You can't hurt him, Cato. Lay a hand on him, and I will take your daughter away."

I didn't appreciate the threat. It only escalated my rage. "You must think very little of me to assume I would hurt someone you consider a friend. Seems out of character for a man who retrieved your father's body so you could bury him properly." If she wanted to throw shit in my face, I could do the same to her.

Siena gave me a cold look before she walked out.

Now I was left alone with Crow Barsetti, the renowned winemaker who lived farther west in Tuscany than I did. "I know your story. I know you were a powerful arms dealer before the Skull Kings took over. Now you've disappeared into the countryside to make wine and spend time with your family. I understand the lesson Siena is trying to teach me."

"Yet, you refuse to learn it."

My eyes narrowed on his face, shocked that this man had the balls to speak to me that way.

"I see the way you look at her." He ignored the glare of rage I threw at him. "It's the way my son-in-law looks at my daughter, and my son looks at his wife. It's the way I look at my wife—even though I've been married to her for over thirty years. You love her."

"That's pretty obvious."

"But it's not obvious why you aren't being the man she deserves. A man can't say he loves a woman unless he's willing to give her everything she needs. That's why a man is so choosy when looking for the right woman. Because a real man knows the sacrifices he'll have to make once he says those words. We won't sacrifice just for anyone. Only someone we can't live without. Siena is clearly that person to you, yet you won't do the right thing. That's irresponsible, if you ask me."

This guy had a lot of nerve. "Siena said you were going to share your life story, not provoke me."

"You know my life story. You know I sacrificed everything the second my wife became pregnant. I knew we would never be safe until we gave up everything. And we were happy for a long time. When my son grew up, he got involved in the bullshit I tried to protect him from...and then the cycle started all over again. Men are easily attracted to ambition, money, and power—but nothing good ever comes from it. I was exactly the same way when I was your age. All I wanted was pussy, money, and power. But once I met that right woman...it all turned to bullshit. I wouldn't trade my quiet life in the countryside for all those years of power. Never. It's hard to make that transition, I understand. But your family will always be at risk until you do. You're arrogant enough to think you can keep them safe, but you can't. Someone will outsmart you someday... and you'll lose everything."

I loved my daughter so much, and I would die if anything ever happened to her. She couldn't even talk yet, and I already had a connection with her. When I stopped by Siena's home to see Martina, I was nearly brought to tears when she was in my arms. She stopped crying the second I held her—and I knew that was because of me.

"Is it really worth the risk, Cato?" This man had walked through the door and immediately patronized me, but there was something about him that prevented me from retaliating. "You miraculously found the woman you love and have a daughter together. Does anything else really matter?"

"You've made your point, Crow."

"I hope I did. Siena is a good kid. She's been through a lot. I used to be friends with her father, and I saw him make the same mistakes you're making now. He thought he was invincible...until his luck ran out. You could ask him if he has any regrets...but he's stuck in a grave with his wife."

I couldn't even contemplate the idea of Siena being dead, because it made my hands shake. I loved her more than I loved myself. I loved Martina more than anything else in the world, including Siena.

Crow stared at me for a while. "Money doesn't matter, Cato. When you're sitting at the dinner table with your wife and kids...you'll see that it doesn't make a difference. Family is the only thing that matters."

———

I arrived at Siena's house later that evening. All the lights were on in the windows, and my men were spread around the perimeter to make sure no one crossed the property line without permission.

My eyes lingered on the front door, and I remembered all the nights I would stop by unannounced. I'd pick the lock and help myself inside like I owned the place—like I owned her. Then I'd take her body well into the night, coming inside her as much as I could because it gave me more pleasure than anything else in life. Her home was cozy and comfortable, possessing a charm my estate could never replicate.

Probably because it was filled with her presence.

I walked up to the door, and instead of letting myself inside, I knocked.

"It's open," she called from within.

I stepped inside and heard Siena washing the dishes in the kitchen. The faucet turned off, and she walked back into the living room to greet me. She didn't seem surprised to see me, like she'd been expecting me all night.

"Where is she?" I wasn't here for Martina, but I wanted to ask anyway.

"She's asleep in her room. You can see her if you want, but try not to wake her up. It took me forever to get her down..."

Because she didn't like it here. She wanted to see both of us together, to see us happy again. She was just a baby, but she picked up on the moods in the room. I'd promised her

I would never leave her, that I would come home every night. I'd already broken that promise.

Siena didn't come close to me. She purposely kept space between us, like we were strangers rather than lovers. "I'm sorry I asked Crow to stop by. I just thought...maybe he could give you his spin on things."

"You really want me to quit, then?"

She sighed, like the question pained her. "I just want us to be safe." Her hand moved over her stomach, just the way she did when she was pregnant. "This is the only way to accomplish that."

My eyes lingered on her hand, the way she clutched herself.

"I love you." She said the words with watery eyes. "I miss you. I want us to be a family again. But I can't risk anything happening to our children. If that ever happened, I would never forgive you..."

I wouldn't forgive myself. I stepped closer to her, still looking at her stomach. "Baby?"

She lifted her gaze to look at me.

My hand moved over hers as my pulse quickened in my throat. My breath came out shaky as the possibility popped into my mind. "Are you pregnant?"

She didn't answer, but she didn't need to. Her watery eyes told me everything.

"We're having another baby." Both of my hands moved to her stomach. She was flat like she used to be, but knowing there was more life inside her excited me all over again. "That's...great."

"Is it?" she whispered. "We're having another baby, but we aren't a family."

"Of course we're a family—"

"Not if we're apart. Not if you won't do everything you possibly can to protect us. You don't deserve us if you're unwilling to do the right thing." She stepped back so my hands would slip away. More tears emerged from her eyes.

"Siena—"

"I don't want to hear you talk if you're just going to say the same thing."

"I'm not."

She let out the breath she'd been holding, the hope entering her gaze like a beacon.

I bowed my head as I collected my thoughts, trying to think of a starting point. I lifted my gaze again to look her in the eye. "I told you my company has turned me into a man. It molded me, shaped me. It's my identity. Without it,

I didn't know what or who I was. I would just be an ordinary man...but then I realized that's the version of me you love anyway. That without that company, I'm still me. I'm still the powerful, rich man who made his own way in life. Even if I give everything to Bates, it'll always be part of me. But it's time to put it up in the past and think about the future. I would be a terrible father if I continued on my same path and assumed there wouldn't be consequences. I don't want to be like your father, Siena. I don't want to make those mistakes...and I won't."

She breathed a sigh of relief, her hand moving over her stomach again. "Good..."

"So I'll give you what you want."

She wiped her tears away, tears of happiness.

"But I want something in return."

"Anything," she whispered. "I'll give you anything you want, Cato."

I reached into my pocket and pulled out the ring, the ring I'd wanted her to wear a few weeks ago. Sleek, elegant, and simple, it was perfect for her. I held it up to her, the band squeezed between my thumb and forefinger. "Put this on. Never take it off." I grabbed her left hand and slipped the ring onto her finger, not waiting for an answer.

She smiled through her tears, her bottom lip quivering. "I promise." She extended her hand to admire the ring before she moved into my chest and kissed me. Her fingers dug into my hair as she kissed me hard, like she'd been fantasizing about this moment forever. "I know you want to see Martina, but—"

I stripped off my jacket and loosened my tie. "I'll see her in the morning."

————

Her ankles were locked together behind my back as her fingers dug into my hair. She moaned every time I thrust deep inside her, having already reached her climax a minute after we started. "Cato...I love you."

I was already so hard for her, but now I got a little harder. She was pregnant with our second child, so she became even more irresistible. Now, she was whispering her love for me, saying my name with the kind of sexiness other women couldn't pull off. "I love you too, baby." Two weeks had come and gone without this. Two weeks too long. I wanted this every night for the rest of my life, even if I had to give up everything to have it.

She grabbed my ass and pulled me deep inside her. "Come inside me." She looked into my gaze as she waited, her lips open with her deep breathing. A sex-crazed look was in her eyes, like she wanted to get off on the feeling of my come. "Please..." She guided my strokes, making them smooth and long.

I moved deep inside then released, dumping all of my seed with a groan so loud it would probably wake up Martina. But I didn't care in that moment. I wanted to fill my woman while she wore my diamond ring on her finger.

"Yes..." Siena squeezed her thighs around my waist as she enjoyed the feeling of my come inside her. "That felt so good."

I kissed both of her tits before I slowly pulled out of her. I lay beside her, feeling all the stress leave my body now that I was reunited with her. I hadn't jerked off once because I'd been too depressed. Now we were reunited—in the sexiest way possible.

And we had another baby on the way.

I placed my hand over her flat stomach. She'd just gotten back into shape, but now that belly would get big all over again. The bigger she got, the more it would turn me on. Then we would have two babies crying throughout the night.

I looked forward to it.

We were both hot and sweaty, but that didn't stop me from holding her. I hiked her leg over my hip so I could bring us close together. My arm clung to her lower back, and I rested my face close to hers.

Now everything felt right.

I was a whole again.

And I didn't have any regrets about the decision I had made.

"Cato?"

"Yes, baby?"

"When did you want to get married?"

"Honestly, I haven't put any thought into it at all. Why?"

"Well, I don't want to be humungous when I get married..."

"What does that mean?" Even when she was eight months pregnant, I hadn't considered her to be humungous. I considered her to be my beautiful, very pregnant, lady.

"Could we get married soon? Like next week?"

"Is that enough time to plan a wedding?"

"I thought we would just go to the town hall and then have a nice dinner somewhere."

I always thought women wanted a fancy wedding, especially since I could throw the biggest wedding of the century. "You don't want a wedding?"

"What for?" she asked. "We aren't close with that many people. It's just about us anyway."

"But you need to get a dress made."

"I already have a dress."

"You do?" asked.

"My mama's." She looked at my lips as she smiled at me. "I've always wanted to wear it."

It was the sweetest thing I'd ever heard her say. Made me wish I'd met her sooner, that way I could have protected her parents from their untimely deaths. "That'll be nice."

"I think so too."

"But you really want to do something so simple as going to the town hall?"

She shrugged. "I honestly don't care where we do it, but planning something elaborate seems unnecessary. We already live together and have a daughter together. I care more about being husband and wife than the actual wedding. That's what I'm excited for."

When she painted a picture like that, I knew I wanted it too. "That sounds good to me."

"So, we'll go to the town hall than have dinner together."

"How about we have dinner under the stars like last time?" I asked. "We can have our first dance. Have our privacy. And this time, I don't have to worry about you rejecting me because you'll already be my wife."

She chuckled. "Sounds smart."

"Then it's a plan."

———

Bates sat across from me, unable to wipe the smirk off his face. "I'm glad you came to your senses." He signed the sheet then passed it to me.

I clicked my pen then added my signature to the bottom. "Siena is too."

"Because you were being a huge asshole." He signed the next paper and handed it over.

"Yes...I'm aware." I added my signature.

We kept up the system, getting through all the legal documents we needed to sign to get my name off all the official paperwork. I wanted the public to believe I'd really stepped aside, and the best way to do that was to make it official in the eyes of the law.

"You think you can handle all this?" I asked.

Bates scoffed. "I did most of the work anyway."

I glared at him.

"Okay, maybe I didn't. But I know I can always call. So, what are your plans? Going to open a new business?"

I shrugged. "I've got another baby on the way, so I'll probably just stay home for a while."

Bates stopped signing and gave me an incredulous look. "Wait, you guys are having another baby?"

I nodded. "Siena told me last night."

"No way. Congratulations. Shit, two babies? One right after another?"

"Yep. I want a third, but I don't think she'll go for it."

"Good thing you quit. It would have been impossible to work and have two young kids at home."

"Siena could have handled it, but I'm glad to be a part of it. I like being a father... It's nice."

Bates didn't tease me for the comment. "I think fatherhood suits you. Our dad was a piece of shit, but you're father of the year. It's funny how things work out sometimes."

"I think you'd be a good father too."

He laughed like I'd made a joke. "No kids for me. I'll stick to condoms."

"Well, one day, you'll ditch the condoms. And if an accident happens...don't worry about it too much."

"I'm not stupid enough to get into that situation in the first place." He signed an entire stack of papers then pushed it toward me. "But good thing it worked out well for you."

"Really well." I added all my signatures to the papers then pushed them back. "The place is officially yours. Don't fuck it up."

"I'll try," he said. "I'll wire your money later."

"Alright." I was officially retired. I had my billions, and now I had nothing to do with it. I already owned my house, and my pregnant fiancée didn't want to travel anywhere while the kids were so young. It was time to settle down for the quiet life Crow swore I would love. "I guess I should head home, then."

"Yep." Bates rose to his feet then came around the table. He did something we hardly ever did and pulled me in for a hug. "I'm proud of you."

"For handing over everything to you?" I asked with a smirk. Now Bates had everything, the entire company to run however he wanted. He was officially richer than me, and he would probably gloat about it.

"No." He clapped me on the shoulder before he pulled away. "For being happy."

26

SIENA

I left my house for good this time—and decided to sell it.

I knew I wouldn't be needing it anymore.

After digging through the boxes in the attic, I found the item I was looking for. Pearl white and made of satin, it hadn't collected dust all these years because it'd been perfectly preserved. I felt the material in my fingertips and tried not to cry.

I wished my mother were here for this.

I carried the dress back downstairs where Landon was waiting for me.

"You got it?" He placed his hands on my hips as he helped me to the ground. Then he pushed the door back into the ceiling.

"Here it is." I held it out for him. "It's beautiful, huh?"

"It's definitely got a distinct style…"

My parents got married twenty-something years ago, so the style was much different then than it was now. "That's what I like about it. It's unique, special. And Mama looked so beautiful in it."

My brother gave me an affectionate look. "You'll look beautiful too."

"Thanks, Landon." I placed it on the couch and took a look around the house. "I'm selling the place. Not much reason to keep it anymore."

"Makes sense. But I have a better idea." He examined the living room and the kitchen before he turned back to me. "Give it to me. You're going to be a billionaire tomorrow, so it's not like you need the money. And the house stays in the family."

"Not a bad idea."

"Plus, you don't have to move all this stuff."

"Well, you aren't being hunted anymore, so you don't have to lay low. You could get a better place."

"But I don't have a job." He crossed his arms over his chest. "So living somewhere for free would be ideal. And, more importantly, I bought you a house in France that you couldn't stand for more than two months. So, you owe me."

I rolled my eyes. "You don't have to guilt me. You know I want you to have it. Maybe you could meet a nice girl and shack up here."

"Or many not so nice girls..."

I swatted his arm playfully. "So, I'll see you tomorrow."

"Am I giving you away? Is there something I need to know?" He walked with me to the door.

"No. We're just going to the town hall and signing the paperwork. Nothing fancy. We'll have our fun afterward."

"That doesn't sound romantic."

"But it will be—for us. Since I'm pregnant again, I don't want to wait around until I'm huge again. Last time, I was so uncomfortable and so hideous. I want to get married while I can still see my feet."

"Understandable."

"Then we're going to have dinner at our place."

"Okay, that does sound boring."

"But it'll be a romantic evening under the stars in the backyard. We'll enjoy the summer evening together. Trust me, it'll be nice."

"How nice can it be when your kid is in the house?" He walked out the front door with me, to where one of Cato's cars was waiting.

"That makes it even better."

He glanced at my old car off to the side, the thing I hardly ever drove anymore. "Can I have that too?"

"Geez, you're cheap."

He shrugged. "If you aren't going to use it, why not? You'll probably get a Ferrari or something."

I laughed. "I can't see myself in a Ferrari. Cato will probably never let me drive my own car again."

"Then I should definitely take it."

"It's not really your style. It's cheap and dusty."

He examined the car, seeing the dirt covering the paint and the windows. "With a little attention, it'll look brand new."

"Alright, it's yours. You want my old job too?"

"No," he said with a chuckle. "I'll find something else. But for now, I don't mind retirement."

"When Cato opens a new business, I can get you a position there."

He shook his head. "No. I'm not interested in a handout."

I gave him an incredulous look then stared at the car and the house. "Really?"

"It's different with you. You're family."

I headed to the car and watched one of Cato's men open the back door. "After tomorrow, Cato will be family too."

———

Our wedding day wasn't traditional in any way whatsoever.

We decided to get married at the town hall with a few friends and family members before we returned to our house for a private dinner. It wasn't fancy, but it was certainly special to us.

We agreed to see each other for the first time just before we left for the town hall. He would wait at the bottom of the stairs for me, and I would make my grand appearance walking down all those flights of stairs in my mama's wedding dress.

I wore the bracelet Cato gave to me, along with pearl earrings and a pearl necklace. My mother had been a classy woman, so her dress was classy too. I stepped out of my bedroom and reached the top stair, my eyes immediately looking for Cato at the bottom.

There he stood, in a deep blue suit with a matching tie. His eyes had been focused on my position because he'd been waiting for this moment for a long time. The second he looked at me, his eyes homed in further, and the corner of his mouth rose in a smile. Showing the boyish charm I loved, his eyes sparkled with love.

I gripped the rail as I moved down to the bottom, keeping my eyes on his the entire time. He was the last man I'd expected to fall in love with, and the last man I'd expected to trust so deeply. And he was definitely the last man I'd expected to risk my life for. Now we had a family together, another little one on the way.

A lot had changed in a year.

I reached the bottom floor, and he circled his arms around me. His hands rested on the steep curve in my back, and he pressed his forehead to mine, his eyes on my lips. Time seemed to stop as he held me in the entryway, in no rush to head to Florence to bind our lives together forever. He didn't press his lips to mine to kiss me, probably wanting to wait until I was his wife.

My arms rested in the crook of his, and I enjoyed the silence with him, the hum of love that vibrated between us. Our love had deepened so much, and just when I thought I couldn't love him anymore, I did. He was the father of my children, my protector, and my provider. He was everything to me.

He rubbed his nose against mine. "Let's get married."

Cato arranged for the town hall to be open late so we could have a private ceremony. We signed all the paperwork and exchanged our vows before the clerk married us in the eyes of our friends and family.

It was the same experience many other couples had, but it felt special to me. It seemed like we were the only two people who really loved each other like this.

He cupped my face and locked his eyes on to mine. "I do."

I said the words back. "I do."

He didn't waste any time leaning in and kissing me. It was a soft embrace but one packed with his undying love and devotion. He kissed me like his mother wasn't watching, and my brother could look away if he didn't like it—which he probably did.

Cato rested his forehead against mine when he pulled away. "Mrs. Marino."

"Husband."

He smiled. "I like that." He took my hand and guided me to our family.

Chiara held Martina in her arms, and she handed her over so we could hold her on our special day. "Congratulations, you two."

"Thanks, Mother." Cato kissed her on the cheek.

I held our daughter and looked down into her face. "We're going to miss you. Have fun with Nana. We'll see you in a few days." I kissed her forehead before I handed her to Cato.

He rocked her back and forth gently before he did the same. "We'll see you soon, sweetheart." He handed her back to his mother.

"Let's take some pictures," Chiara said. "That way you can run off and live happily ever after."

———

Cato and Siena have found their happily ever after, but I have another story even more thrilling than this one.

I've been trapped in a loveless marriage so long I've forgotten how to feel anything. Passion. Desire. Joy. I can't leave or ask for a divorce, not when I gave myself to my husband in exchange for someone else's freedom. It's been years now, and he carries on with his affairs and gives me a black eye the second I say something he doesn't like. I've had enough, so I go out to a bar for a drink—and see *him*. Striking blue eyes, cheekbones as sharp as glass, a body of a gladiator, this man is fire. I stare—and he stares back. He buys me a drink, one thing leads to another, and I tell him the truth, that I'm married. "I don't care that you're married. If you're sitting here alone that means your man is a piece-of-shit husband, so you're fair game." **Read The Skull King** to meet Balto, a man far more dangerous than my husband, the Skull King.

———

Check out Penelope's upcoming release!

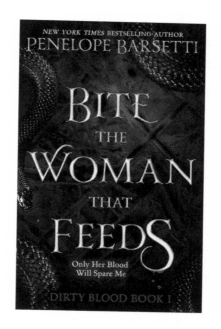

About the book:

Enemies-to-lovers...to unlikely allies...to frenemies with benefits...10/10 spice.

A horrible plague has swept the world.

Millions are sick. More are dying.

Except me. I'm immune.

I'm the only one well enough to defeat this plague and save my people.

Except one problem...

Kingsnake--King of Vampires--is intent on finding me. Without my people to feed on, he'll die. My blood is the only thing that will keep him alive.

He won't stop until he finds me.

Binds me.

And makes me his.

Check out Penelope's upcoming release! **Order your copy now.**